The Three Men Of Gragareth

Norman Harrison

Acknowledgments

My thanks to my editor, publisher and proof readers for all their efforts.

Any remaining failings are entirely my own.

© Copyright Norman Harrison 1994

Norman Harrison asserts the moral right to be identified as the author of this work.

All rights reserved.

No part of this publication may be reproduced, stored in a retrieval system, or transmitted in any form or by any means, electronic, mechanical, photocopying, recording or otherwise, without the prior permission of the author.

First published in 2005

http://www.normanharrison.co.uk

ISBN 1-4116-6823-5

This novel is entirely a work of fiction. The names, characters and incidents portrayed in it are the work of the author's imagination and any resemblance to actual persons, living or dead, events or localities are entirely coincidental.

One

"What the hell?", the rattle of falling stones and a muffled exclamation of pain had disturbed Joss's peaceful stroll home from the pub. His first thought was that it was sheep rustlers. He smiled inwardly at the stupidity of the idea, brought to mind by an earlier conversation with the village gossip. Nobody in their right mind would try to get sheep down that gill at night. The most likely cause would be a party of ramblers who'd overestimated their navigational skills in the dark and were now striving desperately to reach the village pub before closing time.

Concerned in case anyone had been hurt he set off up the track towards Devil's Gill, that gloomy, intimidating ravine in the valley below his farmhouse. It was difficult to see under the overhanging cliffs and the track was rough and difficult to negotiate in the dark. He stopped; the voices were much closer now, and by the row they were making on the rocks he knew they couldn't be very familiar with the route.

Joss waited under the overhang, unsure what to do. The walkers seemed to be moving quite well now. It might just have been the narrowness of the ravine that had amplified the noise. He could see the points of light from numerous flashlights as the group zig-zagged down the final part of the gully towards him. He waited until the first man was about five or six yards away before he stepped out and called, "Everything all right there?"

There was an exclamation of fear and surprise. Before Joss could move, or even formulate a reply, he was blinded by a flashlight shining full in his face, forced roughly back against the cliff and a large pistol thrust into his throat.

"What's up? What the matter?" he croaked, the pistol digging painfully into his Adam's apple.

"Keep still and don't move!", barked his assailant.

Joss was aware of other people milling around him, and then he had another shock. He recognised a familiar voice. He screwed his head round sideways, for once in his life relieved to hear the voice of the clergyman.

"Mr Bergman! It's me, Joss Warrendale", he gasped, "What's going on?"

Bergman came nearer and looked at him coldly, "A little mistake, I fear on your part, Mr. Warrendale, but one that could be catastrophic," he hissed at his companions, "for you, you fools. Keep the gun on him, he's seen too much, and heard too much for his own good, damn the man."

To say that Joss was surprised at these less-than-devout expressions of annoyance would be to totally understate the case however, he felt it prudent not to make any comment just at the moment. In fact, this unexpected train of events right on his own doorstep had disturbed his usual imperturbable nature rather more than he would have cared to admit.

"Bring him with us for the time being until we sort things out", Bergman ordered brusquely. "We can't wait here any longer."

"I can't come with you", Joss protested, "my wife's expecting me home anytime."

"You'll do exactly as you are told, Mr.Warrendale, or you will not be doing anything, ever again", was Bergman's chilling response. Joss was well aware of the menace in the well-modulated voice. "Get him moving and shoot him if he tries to get away."

Joss guessed there were five or six men in the group but he couldn't be sure in the gloom of the overhanging cliffs. He didn't know what was happening; he guessed it was something to do with what old Mrs Thornton had been on about, 'smugglers in the night' she'd said; an idea which had caused him great amusement at the time. He should have listened to the old gossip.

Joss's thoughts were rudely interrupted by the pistol jabbed in his back and with a man on each arm he was marched back down the track to the village. The moonlight shafted eerily through the overhanging trees and added to the unreality of the situation as Joss stumbled along trying to make sense of the evening's events.

It hadn't started too well, he recalled. He'd had a bit of a tiff at the farm with Dorcas, nothing serious, just a mild disagreement really. She'd wanted him to see if the lambs in the bottom pasture were all right before he went to the local, whereas he'd wanted to get down to the 'Flying Horseshoe' as soon as possible. He had gone out of his way to check-up on the lambs anyway, on his way down; of course they were all right, he knew they would be.

The evening had been warm and languorous, the sort of mid-summer evening he particularly enjoyed. The heat of the day had passed but there was a warm stillness about the valley. The pastures were lush, the trees in full leaf, wild flowers flourished profusely in the hedgerows. In fact the natural world was in its full abundance. Joss had paused by the lakeside to appreciate the tranquility of the place; the blue smoke from his pipe hung about his head in delicate layers, seemingly reluctant to disperse. He'd felt at peace with the world and very grateful to be a part of it.

He now recalled that he'd actually passed the parson on his way down, but it had been just a hurried greeting and an even quicker farewell. Joss had never much liked the man, even though he'd been a frequent visitor to the village over the last few months. Bergman had asked him his name and then made some clever remark about Joshua being so trusted by the Lord that he'd been chosen to lead the people of Israel, or something like that. Joss had been too eager to keep moving than to actually bother about what the chap had been saying. Joss however, had wondered at the time where Bergman was going at that time of night. An evening constitutional he'd assumed, quite erroneously, he thought wryly, in view of what had since happened.

The group stopped by the church on the outskirts of the village and a scarf was wrapped around Joss's mouth. From there Bergman went on alone whilst the rest of the men waited in the shadows. Joss could see the lights from the gas lamps filtering through the curtained windows of the cottages in the main street. Old Granny Thornton was still up he noted. He wished to God she would twitch the net curtains tonight. The man close to him seemed to read Joss's thoughts because the barrel of the gun moved up and pressed into the top of his neck behind his right ear, the cold metal sending a sudden shiver down his back.

"Try nothing stupid, my friend", warned the man holding the gun.

Five minutes later a large black saloon car appeared out of the gloom and drew quietly alongside the waiting group. A Mercedes-Benz, Joss noted, as he was bundled into the back between two men. The fourth man sat next to the driver and the motor car purred away down the main street; there was no sign of the parson.

In fact, there wasn't much sight of anything else for Joss that night because as soon as the car had started, with one rough movement the gag over his mouth had been forced up into an effective blindfold.

Joss forced himself to concentrate on the route the vehicle was taking. He felt the car going over the humped-backed bridge over the beck and then north up the main road. None of the men spoke; the large, comfortable limousine swept smoothly through the night.

After about ten minutes the car slowed down and turned sharply to the right. A short distance and it began to climb steeply and the driver had to change down into a lower gear. Ah, thought Joss, either Chapel-le-Dale or Kingsdale. I'll know for sure if we go down the other side. But they didn't go down the other side, ten minutes later they were shaken around as the car bumped and lurched onto a rough track. The driver cursed and stopped the car.

"You walk the rest of the way", he said peremptorily.

Joss was dragged out of the car, his arms forced behind his back and his wrists handcuffed together. He heard the Mercedes reverse and turn around, then the noise of its engine fading into the distance.

For the next half hour he was pushed and pulled over an uneven and rutted track. The more Joss stumbled and staggered, the more his captors grumbled and cursed. They passed through a number of gates and the cooler air on his faced convinced him that he was high on the slopes above Kingsdale. Probably the Turbary Road, he decided. This was an ancient drovers track which ran along a flat shelf-like projection above the valley.

It was a relief to everyone when they reached their destination. Joss had been dragged off the track to his left and steadied as they descended a rocky outcrop. He could hear the sound of running water and felt the splash of it on his feet as they crossed a shallow beck. He felt the touch of some soft material as he moved through a rocky opening and then the dank underground smell of a cave system enveloped him. He was pushed to the ground and curtly told to stay there.

"We've had to bring a prisoner with us", one of the men explained to someone already in the cave. "He's seen too much. Brigante One says we have to keep him here until it's over."

"How long will that be?" Joss asked boldly. He was feeling considerably less worried about his personal safety now. He reasoned that had they been going to kill him they would have already done so. This area was so riddled with caves and potholes, a body could remain undiscovered for years, perhaps for ever.

"About a week at the most, possibly less." The voice was quiet and controlled. Joss thought he detected the slightest trace of an Irish accent.

"I can't stay here a week", Joss objected. "I've my wife to look after, and the farm, I've too much to do. I'll be missed, they'll all be looking for me."

"Your wife will be all right as long as you do as you're told; your farm can wait until you get back."

"You promise my wife will be all right?"

"You have my word, as an officer and a gentleman," the Irish voice assured him. "Can we take off the blindfold and the handcuffs now? Have we a gentleman's agreement?"

Joss nodded his head slowly, he wasn't too sure what credentials the Irishman had in terms of gentlemanly behaviour. Anyway, Joss thought, he didn't have much choice so he might as well go along with him, and hope for a chance to get away later.

The cave, Joss noted, was quite spacious and relatively warm. It was about the size of a narrow room, perhaps four yards long and two to three yards wide. It was curtained at each end and a hissing tilly lamp hanging on the wall cast a dim pale light over the interior.

Joss studied the face of the man sitting opposite; aged about forty, slim build, dark hair, clean-shaven, lively intelligent eyes. A man you could trust? That, he was not too sure about. The Irishman was wearing the same kind of green overalls as the others, but on his head he wore a woollen hat pulled down over his ears, whereas the others wore green military-style forage caps.

Noticing Joss's scrutiny the Irishman looked at him with a level gaze and said not unkindly, "She'll be all right. We have a job to do here. When it's done you'll be released, so make yourself comfortable." He indicated one of a number of bedding rolls in the corner, "That's your bed for the night, so I suggest you settle down now. Goodnight and sleep well."

Joss sorted out his bed roll, took off his boots and coat and wriggled into a sleeping bag fully clothed. No point in making a fuss this time o' night, he reasoned. His unaccustomed midnight hike and his previous alcoholic intake produced an immediate drowsiness. He tried to follow the few scraps of conversation; they were talking about 'the trip over', and 'getting down in one piece' and 'best not to upset Brigante One', but thereafter it all became disjointed and, in spite of his efforts to stay awake and listen, he fell into a deep and undisturbed sleep.

Two

King's Cross Station, 4th July 1939

Jack sprinted along the edge of the platform alongside the moving train; he could vaguely hear the shouts of the ticket collector at the barrier far behind him. With one desperate lunge he grasped the handle of the nearest third class compartment door, wrenched it open, flung his suitcase inside and threw himself in after it. Absolutely exhausted, he leaned against the side of the door, his chest heaving and his face contorted as he desperately gasped for breath.

After some such seconds of laboured breathing he regained his composure and looked furtively around, embarrassed in case his unorthodox and precipitous entry had been noticed by any other passengers. It had; a gentleman in the compartment facing the corridor door was looking across with utter disdain on his face. As Jack caught his eye the man quickly looked away and raised his copy of The Times in front of his face, as though to shield himself from any further contact with such a ruffian. Just a little bit uncharitable for a parson, Jack thought, as he self-consciously straightened his tie and smoothed his ruffled hair. He moved slowly along the corridor in search of a more welcoming compartment.

"Bloody stuffed shirt," he muttered beneath his breath, annoyed at himself for being affected by the man's disapproval.

The next compartment appeared to be completely full of giggling, semi-hysterical schoolgirls, obviously intent upon having a jolly summer vacation. Jack cringed and moved hurriedly on to the next.

He paused outside the third compartment; this looked decidedly promising. The sole occupant, sitting by the window in the far corner, was a smartly-dressed young lady in her late twenties, Jack guessed. She glanced up from the book on her knee as Jack slid open the door.

"Excuse me, do you mind if I join you? I've been looking for a quiet compartment."

"Not at all," replied the young lady in a refined voice, fixing Jack with a pair of steady blue eyes which sent shock waves through his nervous system.

"Thank you very much," Jack mumbled, as he selected a seat on the other side to the girl and threw his suitcase on to the rack opposite.

The girl had returned to her reading and this allowed Jack to observe his travelling companion a little more closely, albeit covertly. A slim, attractive girl, perhaps a year or two younger than Jack, fair hair cut rather short, and the aforesaid blue eyes. She was dressed rather formally in a dark grey business suit with a white blouse trimmed with lace at the collar.

Jack stared out of the window for a while watching the back gardens of suburbia flashing past. Then he turned his attention to the interior of the compartment; the net luggage racks, the girl's suitcase on the rack above him, the sepia coloured photographs of the British countryside above the seats. Jack observed with some delight that he was sitting directly opposite a striking photograph of Ingleborough, that instantly recognisable profile in a cloud-filled backdrop, taken from somewhere over on the far side, probably on the road to Wensleydale.

Quite a coincidence, he thought, remembering his own destination, and the hectic rush he'd had that morning to catch the 10.25 from King's Cross.

He reached into the inside pocket of his jacket and extracted the letter he'd received by that morning's post. He studied the envelope, postmarked at Leeds, 5.30 pm on the 1st July 1939. It was addressed, in the neat precise hand which he had immediately recognised as belonging to his

Aunt Dorcas, to Mr. Jack Warrendale, 42 Leyton High Street, Leyton, East London. Jack unfolded the letter and re-read it slowly.

High Top Farm, Langham,

Nr. Settle,

Yorkshire

30th June 1939

Dear Jack,

I hope you are keeping well. I am writing to you in some urgency because I am very worried about your Uncle Joss. He went into the village the day before yesterday and he has not come back yet. I know he does sometimes stay over at one of his friend's houses but only if the weather is bad and he always manages to let me know. I was so worried I sent the lad down to look for him. He couldn't find any trace so I informed P.C.Bainbridge. He came up to see me on his bicycle yesterday tea-time but he was not able to give me any information whatsoever. He's a very nice man, as you know, and he took all the details and told me not to worry as there would be quite a simple explanation. But I am worried Jack as Joss wouldn't leave the farm for so long if he could help it. You know what he's like when it comes to work. I thought I'd better write and let you know straight away.

Best love,

Aunty Dorcas

Jack folded the letter thoughtfully, a worried expression on his face. He could picture his uncle clearly; a well-built, florid-faced farmer, of real yeoman stock. Stolid, reliable, a man of his word, and a descendant of a family which had been respected in the small rural community around Langham for generations.

Jack was disturbed from his reverie by gradually becoming aware that the girl in the opposite corner was looking at him. He met her gaze with some embarrassment and felt his face flushing; he was unsure how long she'd been watching him for one thing, and he didn't know how much she'd been able to read in his expression for another. His discomfort was only momentary however because the girl smiled sympathetically.

"Bad news?" she asked, her voice quiet and concerned.

Jack smiled ruefully, at himself really, for making his feelings so transparent.

"I'm afraid so," he replied, gaining in confidence, "It's a letter from my aunt telling me that my uncle has gone missing from home, without any apparent explanation. I'm on my way up to Yorkshire now to see what I can do."

"I'm sorry to hear that," she said. "I hope everything turns out all right."

"Oh I'm sure he'll be all right. He's a very fit man for his age. At the moment I'm more concerned about my aunt. She's not so active nowadays and can't get out on her own. That's why I was so desperate to get this particular train; I've been rushing about all morning", he finished rather lamely, at a loss how to proceed, without telling his life story, and yet wishing desperately to continue the conversation.

"Are you going far?" was the best he could come up with before the opportunity was lost.

"Yes, as matter of fact I'm going up to Yorkshire too, on holiday," she added, almost as an afterthought. "My parents live in Leeds and I haven't been up to see them for some time."

"Do you work in London, then?" Jack enquired.

"Well, you might say so," she said with a quick smile. "I'm in the Civil Service, actually."

Jack was impressed but unsure how to continue without appearing to be too presumptuous. He smiled understandingly and nodded his head, inwardly cursing at himself for being so socially inept in this situation. He resumed his study of the carriage interior with all the earnestness of someone attempting to commit the entire contents to memory. The luggage label on the girl's suitcase above him had caught his eye and he was in the awkward position of trying to read the address without noticeably raising his head from the horizontal, when the girl spoke again.

"Do you work in the City?"

"I er, yes er I do as a matter of fact," he answered hesitantly, as he desperately thought how best to describe his stultifying, totally mind-blowing, boring job in the office. "I'm in shipping," he started. "A shipping agents actually, we arrange the transport for manufacturers all over the Home Counties," he added rather lamely.

"That sounds terribly interesting," a clear invitation in the girl's voice for Jack to continue.

"Well, it's not really," Jack demurred, a clear vision in his mind of the dark Dickensian office; one high stool, a sloping desk and a monotonous mound of invoices and consignment notes to work through every day. "I used to work in Leeds," he said, eager to dismiss the London image, "but the boss wanted me to get some experience in the London office. I've only been there six months. I can't say I'm keen on it - I like the countryside too much and I'm looking forward to getting back up north next year."

"I saw you looking at that picture of the mountain on the wall," she said, indicating the photograph opposite Jack. "Have you been there?"

"Oh yes, lots of times," he answered, glad at last to be on a topic which he knew a great deal. "Ingleborough it's called, it's just about in the back garden of my Uncle's farm."

"I'd love to go up there; it looks really dramatic."

"It is, it's lovely. From the summit you can see all over the limestone pavements and across to Kingsdale and Whernside. Further to the north you can see the hills of the Lake District and, and round to the west you look out over Morecambe Bay. On clear days you can even see the Isle of Man." He paused there, feeling he was being carried away by his enthusiasm for the area.

The girl, however, seemed genuinely interested and continued, "How fascinating; where does one start the climb?"

"Well, there's a number of routes up there, you can start from any side. Probably the easiest way is from near my uncle's farm at Langham. It only takes about an hour at the most, going steadily, from there to the summit."

"I hope I get chance to give it a try this holiday."

"Well er, if I can help at all I'd be delighted to offer my services as your guide if you like," Jack blurted out, quite surprised at his own effrontery. "That is if I can sort out my uncle's disappearance fairly easily," he added, remembering, almost guiltily, why he was making the journey.

"That's very kind of you," she said warmly and smiling at him. "By the way, my name is Ruth. Ruth Lancaster.

"How do you do? I'm Jack Warrendale." Jack stood up, reached over and shook hands with her. His heart missed a beat as he felt the cool soft touch of her hand and he felt the colour rise in his cheeks again. He sat down opposite her by the window, hoping she hadn't noticed his temporary embarrassment. If she had she didn't show it, and Jack soon recovered his composure and settled back in his seat a warm feeling of goodwill infusing his whole body. Things were certainly improving after the day's terrible beginning.

Old Jonesy, the chief clerk, had not been at all pleased when Jack had telephoned him and told him he'd been called up to Yorkshire in some urgency and that he wouldn't be in the office for a week at least. Anyway, here he was travelling north with a most charming companion, who, for some reason, seemed to find him interesting, and what's more, actually fancied climbing Ingleborough with him.

They chatted pleasantly for some time and Jack was feeling very much more at ease now. Initially he had felt rather overawed by Ruth's refined speech, expensive clothes and obvious sophistication. As they talked he was impressed by her pleasant easy-going manner and the way in which she seemed to accept him for what he was; an ignorant country bumpkin, thought Jack to himself wryly.

"Would you like a drink? Tea or coffee perhaps," asked Jack when there was a lull in the conversation. "I could nip up to the buffet and get some."

"Yes, thank you. I'd love a cup of tea. We'll be coming into Peterborough soon and the train might fill up a bit there."

"Righto! Be back in a minute." Jack got up and slid back the door, smiled at Ruth, and went out into the corridor, closing the door behind him.

He steadied himself on the handrail as the train lurched round a bend. He noticed that the schoolgirls in the next compartment were still giggling as he straightened up and then made his way forward to the buffet car.

There were a couple of people in front of him in the queue and he had to wait a few minutes before it was his turn to be served. Jack was just in the process of ordering tea and cakes for the two of them when the train slowed its pace and, in a very short time and with a good deal of harsh grinding, drew into a station and pulled up alongside the platform spewing out steam from apparently every pore. As it cleared Jack saw the station sign. Peterborough already? Doing well, he thought. Doesn't seem two minutes since we left Kings Cross. His thoughts returned to his attractive travelling companion. Very, very nice, he mused and blessed the good fortune that had put him in that particular carriage on the train.

To Jack's dismay he was kept waiting longer than he expected; the attendant had to boil some more water for the tea. The activity on the platform had ceased when Jack was finally served; he heard the guard's whistle and he staggered and grabbed the counter as the train made its first shuddering movement.

Balancing the teapot, sugar basin, milk jug, biscuits, cups and saucers on the tray he carefully edged his way back along the corridors. It was a nerve-wracking trip for Jack, and a test of his sophistication he thought; to be found on the corridor with a pile of broken crockery and an assortment of damp biscuits would be the ultimate disgrace. However, by judicious use of the handrail and by rolling with each lurch of the train after the manner of any cabin boy caught in a gale in the Bay of Biscay, he managed to reach his own compartment with the tray and contents intact.

He was congratulating himself on this achievement when he realised the compartment was empty. He slid open the door, went in and placed the tray on the window table. The girl's book was open on the seat where she'd been sitting and, looking up, he saw her suitcase was still on the rack. Probably gone to the toilet. He smiled, and gazed idly out of the window for a time. He poured out a cup of tea for himself, added one spoonful of sugar and a drop of milk and settled back in his seat. He glanced again at the photograph of Ingleborough, it looked very impressive from that angle, he decided, but quite unmistakable with its distinctive flat summit.

His thoughts returned to the present, where did she go? He looked at his watch, almost unconsciously, and without noticing the time. He must have been back at least ten minutes or so by now. He stood up, opened the door and looked up and down the corridor; nobody in sight. He sighed and went back inside, reaching up to the luggage rack he examined the label tied on the handle:

> *Miss Ruth Lancaster*
>
> *The Arches*
>
> *Moortown Lane*
>
> *Leeds*

Mmm, that sounds very grand, he thought. He was interrupted by the sound of the door opening behind him. He whirled around a smile forming on his face, but his hopes were immediately dashed; it was the ticket inspector.

"Tickets please, sir."

Jack fiddled in the inside pocket of his jacket and produced his ticket. The inspector gave it a cursory glance and handed it back, "Thank you, sir," he said, the phrase used by him so frequently it was just about devoid of meaning, if indeed he was even aware of its use.

"Er.. excuse me," said Jack, as the man was half out of the door. "You haven't by any chance seen a young lady with fair hair and wearing a grey suit, on the train, have you?" He felt stupid as soon as he'd said it, there must be many such women on the train. The inspector looked at him curiously and Jack felt obliged to add, "Oh, she's probably just gone to get washed, it's all right."

The inspector nodded his head, half smiled and closed the door.

Jack, however, was quite worried now, what if she'd been offended by his approaches and moved to another compartment? Probably sitting with that vicar farther back. No, she couldn't have, he reasoned. She wouldn't have left her book and suitcase behind. Anyway, we were getting on well together. She'll be back in a minute. I'll bet she's met someone she knows.

He returned to his seat and poured himself another cup of tea. He picked up the girl's book for the first time, it was a tourist's guide to the Yorkshire Dales. He leafed through a few pages but he was becoming increasingly more anxious and was quite unable to concentrate on the words in front of him.

What should I do now? he wondered. Search the train is the obvious thing to do, he decided. He leapt to his feet full of purpose, and it was at that moment that he realised that his suitcase was not on the rack opposite him.

"Bloody hell !" he exclaimed. He looked around the compartment and under the seats but there was no sign of it anywhere.

"What is going on?" he muttered. Nobody in their right mind would want a case full of dirty washing, that's for sure. Jack was annoyed now; what had seemed so promising initially was fast becoming farcical, and his normal state of equanimity was being seriously disturbed.

He left the compartment, a worried expression on his face; he was going to search every inch of the train until he found her, and his suitcase. The schoolgirls were still in the adjacent compartment, the next one was empty; the vicar had gone.

That's one good thing, anyway, thought Jack, his natural good humour beginning to return. She was not in any other compartment in the carriage and the toilet was showing 'vacant'. He pushed open the door anyway; empty. He crossed the connecting corridor into the last carriage and checked each compartment, there was no sign of the girl at all. The guard's van was the only one left; Jack squeezed between the boxes, bicycles and assorted crates towards the guard's van at the very rear of the train. The elderly guard looked up as Jack approached, it was the same man who had been checking the tickets earlier, Jack noted with some disquiet.

"No, I've not seen no sign of any young lady," he replied in answer to Jack's query, " though a lot of people did get off at Peterborough, you know."

Jack thanked him and threaded his way back through the luggage to the main passenger section.

Where could she be? Perhaps she's got back already and is now wondering where I am. Jack smiled at the thought and rushed back to the compartment. Breathless, but full of hope, he looked through the glass door - no one there. His heart sank. "This is impossible", he groaned to himself.

Jack next went forward and searched the rest of the train, even the first-class compartments, but there was no sign of Ruth.

Back again in his own compartment Jack thought out his next course of action. Ruth's suitcase was still here so from that he deduced that she had not intended to leave the train. He'd better inform the authorities, that'd be the guard in the first place, he decided, and then the Transport Police at the next stop. His mind wrestled with these ideas and with various conjectures about Ruth's disappearance for a long time before he once again made his way to the guard's van and told the official there everything that had happened. The guard listened patiently until Jack had finished but he did not seem to think it anything to worry about unduly.

"It happens all the time, sir. People changing their minds, realising they'd forgotten something, cutting journeys short without warning. There's usually quite a simple explanation, sir. I shouldn't worry about it if I was you." He was, however, at a loss how to explain the suitcase being left behind.

Jack decided he was not going to get very far with the guard so he thanked him for his help and told him that, since he was going to Leeds himself, he would deliver the suitcase to the girl's address.

The journey from then on seemed quite interminable. Jack attempted to read the book on the Yorkshire Dales from time to time, but his mind was preoccupied and he was unable to keep his mind on the subject matter. He finally gave up trying to divert himself and sat staring out of the window, the rhythmic clatter of the wheels on the track a background to his hopes, fears and fantasies.

Three

Leeds Railway Station, 4th July 1939

At last, the Leeds Central station sign appeared in the window. "Thank God for that", muttered Jack as he pulled down Ruth's suitcase, getting some small degree of comfort from that, and also the fact that he was now able to do something constructive after hours of inactivity. He moved to the carriage door long before the train drew to halt, released the window strap and stuck his head out of the window. He half expected Ruth to be waiting on the platform with a welcoming smile; this had been one of his favourite fantasies during the journey. Reality, however, was much more mundane, and disappointing.

He left the train and eagerly scanned the bustling crowd of people heading for the ticket barriers. He handed over his ticket and hurried through to the station concourse but there was no sign of his fellow-traveller anywhere.

Jack had devised plenty of contingency plans on the train. If Ruth was not here to meet him he would take a cab to her house, drop off the suitcase and then come back to the city centre and stay overnight in a bed and breakfast place or cheap hotel. He'd get the early train out to Langham the next morning.

He was lucky and got a taxi straight away, an Austin Ten Cambridge, he noted. One of the diversions in the office had been to study all the latest models of cars which passed the windows. Jack and the other male clerk had become quite knowledgeable in the past few months. The cab driver was a taciturn individual, although he seemed to warm slightly when Jack gave his destination as Moortown and saw the expensive piece of luggage he was carrying.

"Right you are, sir," he said with forced cheerfulness, "we'll be there in about twenty minutes I should think." This obviously took too much out of him because he didn't say another word until the cab drew up outside a pleasant, detached house in a leafy suburb of the city. Jack paid the man and looked over the gate at the extensive lawns and well-kept gardens.

Just a little bit classy, he thought as he composed himself for what might turn out to be a bit of an ordeal. He gripped the suitcase in his right hand and strode up the gravel path towards the front door. He was halted in his tracks by a greeting from the shrubbery behind him.

"Good afternoon! Can I help you?"

Jack spun round to see a white-haired gentleman in a long, loose-fitting cardigan coming towards him from the direction of a garden shed. "I'm Alfred Lancaster," the man continued as he got closer.

"Oh, er... good afternoon, sir. My name is Warrendale, Jack Warrendale, I'm a friend of Ruth's."

"Well, how do you do, young man? I'm Ruth's father." He removed his gardening glove as he spoke and shook hands with Jack warmly. "A friend of Ruth's you say, how is she? Is she well? We haven't seen her for some time, although she does write. In fact we got a letter from her earlier this week."

Jack was wondering how best to explain the unusual situation without causing any undue anxiety. "Well, it's a little unusual is this, sir," he started, "You see this is Ruth's suitcase. She was on her way up to see you but .. but was apparently called away on business at Peterborough, and she left the suitcase with me. I was rather hoping she'd been in touch with you on the telephone and explained the position."

"No.. er, not that I know of, that's very unusual, isn't it? Let's go inside and see if her mother has heard anything. She may have telephoned whilst I've been in the garden."

Ruth's father shepherded Jack through the doorway and into the quite magnificent hallway, at least that's what Jack thought. He'd certainly not seen anything as grand as this in a private house before.

"Come inside, Jack. It's very kind of you to bring Ruth's case here for her."

"Not at all, I was pleased to be able to help," Jack said as his gaze took in the oak-panelled walls and the elegant staircase.

"Amelia!" Ruth's father called, "are you there? We have a visitor, a friend of Ruth's."

A small grey-haired lady entered from a room off the hall. "Oh, good afternoon," she said in a voice which immediately reminded Jack of her daughter. "I've just been doing a bit of baking in the kitchen," she explained, wiping her hands on the blue and white striped pinafore. "Did you say a friend of Ruth's?" her clear blue eyes searching Jack's face for some explanation.

"Yes, we were travelling north on the same train today but she was called back urgently," Jack lied, finding himself becoming immersed rather more deeply in deceit than he wanted. "I thought she might have telephoned and explained."

"Well she might have done, but I've been out in the kitchen garden and I may not have heard it ring."

"Look," interjected Mr Lancaster," you will stay for dinner, won't you? It's not often we get visitors, is it, Amelia? It will be nice to hear about Ruth and her friends."

Oh God, thought Jack, how the hell am I going to get out of this? Whilst he was frantically searching around in his mind for some plausible avenue of escape, his thoughts were interrupted by Mrs Lancaster.

"Do you live in Leeds, Jack?" she asked.

"No," Jack replied, "I'm travelling up to Langham tomorrow."

Jack then explained the reason for his journey, about his uncle's disappearance and the letter which had brought him north so urgently.

When he'd finished Mrs Lancaster took his arm and led him into a sitting room. "You sit down here, dinner will be ready in about twenty minutes and we'd be delighted if you would join us." It was a kind and homely invitation which Jack found that he could not refuse. He was beginning to feel rather fond of this charming couple. He sat for a while in a comfortable arm-chair and studied the tastefully decorated room. He'd just risen to his feet to look more closely at a family photograph on the mantelpiece when Mr Lancaster entered the room.

"Ah, that's a photo of Ruth taken a couple of years ago. That's her sister, Maureen; she's at college in Manchester at the moment, and that's their mother, of course, in the middle," he said indicating the figures on the photograph.

He sat down on the sofa opposite Jack, "Did Ruth say what the business was about?"

"Not exactly," Jack prevaricated. "I gathered it was some important Civil Service business so I didn't enquire too much."

This seemed to satisfy the older man and he settled back and produced his smoking kit from his cardigan pocket. When he'd filled his pipe and got it going to his satisfaction he eyed the horizontal levels of blue smoke hanging in the still air thoughtfully for a moment, before asking Jack about his work in London. They discussed various other topics such as the weather, the political situation, especially the rise in power of the Nazis in Germany. They were interrupted by Mrs Lancaster's voice from the hallway telling them that dinner was ready.

It was a superb home-made meal and Jack, who had not eaten all day, really did it justice. So absorbed was he in eating, in fact, that he found it difficult to join in the general small talk across the table. Mrs Lancaster noted his appreciation with great delight during the meal but demurred at his fulsome praise of her cooking as he put his knife and fork down. "That was the best meal I've had for ages, Mrs Lancaster, thank you very much indeed."

"Get on with you, Jack," she said self-deprecatingly but obviously pleased with the compliment. "By the way, where are you staying tonight? I've been meaning to ask all afternoon."

"I thought I'd go into Leeds and find a bed and breakfast place and catch the early train in the morning."

"Look, why don't you stay here with us? We've plenty of room, in fact, you can have Ruth's old room; the bed-clothes just need airing. We'd be very pleased if you'd stay, wouldn't we, Alfred?" Ruth's father nodded his agreement immediately.

"Yes, that's the sensible thing to do. I'll run you down to the station in the morning, and ", as an afterthought, he added with a smile, " Amelia will see you get a decent breakfast to start with."

Before Jack could begin to express his thanks at their hospitality the strident tone of the telephone from the hall interrupted the conversation. Mrs Lancaster started at the sound and looked at her watch, "Who can that be at this time?"

She went through into the hall and the two men could just hear disjointed snatches of conversation through the open door.

"Oh, hello dear," the men in the dining room could hear the excitement in her voice, " how nice to hear from you."

"It's Ruth on the phone, Alfred!" she shouted through into the dining room. She carried on with the telephone conversation.

"Yes, yes, but..."

"No, there's no need...It's all right, it's here."

"No, here...at home! A young man...Jack Warrendale. He brought it for you. He's here now."

"No, I don't know. Do you want a word with him?

"No? all right then."

"Yes, I suppose so. Langham? Yes.Yes. He's going there tomorrow."

"All right, if you say so. Right love, The Old Crown. Yes. I'll tell him. No. No. I'm sure he won't mind."

"Are you all right, love?"

"Yes, 'bye Ruth. We'll be seeing you soon then? 'Bye, then."

The two men looked expectantly towards the door as Mrs Lancaster came through.

"Is everything all right, dear?" Ruth's father asked, the concern apparent in his voice. Jack had also noticed the worried look on Mrs Lancaster's face as she came into the room.

"Yes, I think so," his wife replied slowly. "At least she said she was, but, if you ask me, she didn't sound like herself at all."

"How do you mean, love?" queried her husband.

"Well, she sounded sort of nervous, tense like, and she didn't seem to want to chat at all."

"What's she doing now?" he asked.

"Oh, she's been delayed on business in the south."

Jack inwardly breathed a sigh of relief. He had been only too well aware that his credibility with her parents would have been seriously undermined if that hadn't checked out.

"Ruth wonders if you wouldn't mind taking her suitcase up to Langham for her, Jack?", Mrs.Lancaster went on. "She's coming up later in the week. She'll be staying at The Old Crown, she says. Do you know it, Jack?"

Jack said he did. As there were actually only two pubs in the village itself there wasn't much difficulty about that. "The Crown's an old coaching inn, Mrs. Lancaster," he explained. "It was on the London-Leeds-Kendal route in the old days. Is Ruth coming up to Langham herself then?" He enquired, trying to contain the eagerness in his voice.

"Well, that's what she said, Jack. Something to do with work but I didn't quite get what." Turning to her husband she added, "She did say she hoped to get a few days with us though, Alfred, when she's finished."

"Ah," he grunted. "We'll find out then what she's up to, I suppose. It'll do her good to have a break, we haven't seen her for months."

Jack couldn't help wondering just exactly what sort of business could take a young lady like Ruth to a small village in the Dales at such short notice. However he thought it politic to keep these thoughts to himself; all being well he'd find out himself later on.

He slept in Ruth's bedroom that night, which he also found rather comforting. In spite of such a limited acquaintanceship he felt he was really getting to know her now. He slept very soundly and was awakened by the sound of birdsong outside the bedroom window, a feature of life he'd sorely missed whilst living in the City. He washed, shaved and dressed and went down to the most enormous cooked breakfast he'd ever seen on one man's plate.

Jack thanked Ruth's parents profusely for their hospitality, and Mrs.Lancaster particularly for the meals, and promised to keep an eye on Ruth and see that she didn't work too hard.

The two men drove down to the station in Mr. Lancaster's beautifully polished dark green Morris Eight Tourer. They shook hands in the station forecourt and Jack hurried off to catch the 10.30 train up to Langham, in fact, to every station up to and beyond. It was the local 'stopper'; it seemed to be more often stationary than actually moving, but on this occasion Jack didn't mind at all. Usually he would have been fuming with frustration, mentally urging the passengers quickly on and off the train at each stop. Today he had all the time in the world; it was a beautiful morning and his mind was full of pleasant possibilities, most of them, it must be said, connected in some way with Ruth Lancaster.

Jack was able to relax in a compartment by himself and reflect on the events of the last two days. Was it only yesterday that he'd met her for the first time? It seemed ages ago. He gloried in the lush greenery of the pastures as the train steamed its way northwards through the rolling countryside.

He took out the book on the Yorkshire Dales that Ruth had been reading yesterday. For the first time he noticed that the corner of the page had been turned down at the chapter on Ingleborough. Mmm, surprising, he thought, remembering Ruth's interest in the mountain. He read for a time but found his attention wandering to the familiar views of the limestone scenery above Settle.

Great to be back, he thought, feeling like taking huge draughts of country air through the carriage window. "To one who has been long in city pent, tis very sweet to look in the fair and open face of heaven." He laughed to himself at the aptness of those lines he'd disliked learning at school. Was it Keats? Shelley perhaps? One of that gang, he couldn't remember which.

All too soon, it seemed, the train was pulling into the small station at Langham. Just looking at the high fells on his right as they drew alongside the short platform gave an immediate lift to Jack's spirits. Familiarity with the place gave him a feeling of confidence; everything was just the same as he remembered it; the old waiting room, the white fence, the pub opposite, Harold Winterburn, the stationmaster, waiting for the tickets. There was a timelessness about places up here, Jack thought to himself, a kind of permanence, which you certainly didn't get in London.

He took down Ruth's suitcase and went on to the corridor. There were very few passengers leaving the train at this stop. Harold smiled a greeting when he saw Jack.

"You'll be worried about your uncle, won't you lad?" he said as he took Jack's ticket.

"Aye, I am that. That's why I'm here. Aunty Dorcas wrote to me about it. You haven't heard owt, have you?"

"Nay, I'm sorry, lad. Nowt at all, but the police have been up from Settle to help Bob Bainbridge with the searching and questioning and whatnot."

Jack remembered Constable Bainbridge all right, he'd kept out of his way for about six months when Jack and two of his pals had pinched a dozen or so apples from the orchard at the back of the policeman's house. That was a good few years ago now, Jack recalled, but he'd never forgotten the long detours they'd made through the fields to avoid the constable in the main street, and the self-induced feeling of being a 'wanted person.' He smiled at the recollection. "I'd better be getting off up to the farm to see if the old lady is all right. I'll be seeing you around."

"Aye, good luck, lad."

Four

Langham, Yorkshire Dales, 5th July 1939

The village of Langham had developed on each side of a small beck; two road bridges and two narrow pack-horse bridges link the two sides. The original Anglo-Saxon settlers, with an inexplicable lack of foresight, sited their settlement over a mile away from the railway station, and Jack had this distance to walk to the village. He'd decided to go straight to his uncle's farm. The matter of Ruth's suitcase could be sorted out afterwards.

Fifteen minutes later he strode up the main street, passing The Old Crown on his right. He followed the beck up the centre of the village, turned left just past the parish church at the head of the main street and a sharp right turn then took him into the woods. He followed the well-worn and familiar track until he came to the lake, pausing there momentarily to watch a pair of tufted ducks go through their diving routine. The next part of the path he always regarded as the last lap. A level walk along the side of the lake, across a short stretch of open ground by the upper reaches of the beck until he reached a gate on his left. This was the lower entrance to his uncle's land and from which the track climbed steeply for a hundred yards or so up to the farmhouse.

The house itself was a solid, grey-stoned structure, softened in places by the ancient orange lichen which had found refuge there. A couple of large barns and three smaller outhouses enclosed the courtyard; it was, by far, one of the oldest buildings in the district. Jack's uncle had often told him about the history of the place and how it had been part of a fortified manor during the time of the monasteries.

As Jack neared the farm buildings, and considered its isolation, he realised just how much he had missed the place and just how serious his uncle's disappearance was. He was not a young man, early sixties probably, his wife was no longer very active and the farm had to be looked after, the sheep on the fellside to be checked, food and other supplies to be brought in. Jack quickened his pace and hurried up the path to the door. He knocked once and went straight inside.

"Hello! Aunt Dorcas? It's me, Jack", there was a warning bark from Jemmy, his aunt's elderly bull terrier. The bark immediately changed to a whimper of delight when she recognised Jack's voice. There was a sudden canine rush across the room, an ecstatic frenzy of tail wagging as both Jack and the dog welcomed the reunion.

His aunt was sitting by the side of the black-leaded Yorkshire range. She had some knitting on her knee but was not actually holding the needles. Her face was sad and looked more careworn than Jack had remembered it. She looked up at the dog's bark and smiled spontaneously when she saw Jack.

"Eee, I'm right glad to see you, Jack. I am that. I didn't know what to do for the best. Neighbours have been right good but they all have their own lives to lead."

"It's all right, Auntie. I'm glad to be here, you know how I love this place, anyway. I'll be able to look after things here and we'll soon find Uncle Joss."

"Oh, I hope so, love. I don't know what he's been up to."

Jack interrupted his Aunt when she appeared about to dwell on the disappearance. "Do you fancy a cup of tea, Auntie?" he said in a lively voice. "I'll just put the kettle on."

"Aye, 'course you'll be wanting something after all your travelling. Your bedroom's all ready for you, I've aired the sheets and had a bit of a dust round."

As they drank their tea in front of the fire Jack told his aunt about the journey up, omitting all except a cursory mention of Ruth; he rightly felt that one disappearance at a time was all his aunt could cope with. Anyway she was keen to tell him what had happened the previous weekend.

"We'd had a bit of a row about the sheep in that bottom pasture, summat and nowt it were. But you know what Joshua's like, he blusters a bit. Said he'd do it straight away, 7 o'clock on a Saturday night, I ask you! He said he'd sort 'em out and then he was off down to t'pub for a quiet drink and I wasn't to wait up." She paused here and looked into the fire. Jack put his hand on her shoulder comfortingly.

"Did you wait up for him?

"No, I didn't," she continued. "I went to bed about ten like I allus do, and I must have dropped off. It wasn't until next morning that I missed him. Even then I thought he'd got up and gone over to the barn. It weren't until young Bert came about nine o'clock, you know Bert, don't you? The lad who comes up to help two days a week."

Jack nodded, he knew Bert well enough and liked the lad. A smiling, round-faced, simple soul, willing to tackle any job that came his way, as long as it was carefully explained to him beforehand.

"Well, I asked Bert if he'd seen him and he hadn't so I sent him off back down the village to make some enquiries. I was very worried even then and when Bert came back with no news at all I were desperate so I just sent Bert down to fetch Constable Bainbridge. He came up on his bicycle about one o'clock and took all the details down in his notebook. He's a nice man is Bob, he said not to worry as he'd started making some enquiries already."

"He said Joss had been in the Flying Dutchman near the station until about ten and then he called in The Crown on the way back. He was with his pals Fred and Ernest, the landlord said he saw 'em go out just before eleven. Fred and Ernest said they'd talked for a bit and the last they saw of Joss was him walking up the main street towards the church. Nobody that they know of has seen him since."

"That's when I wrote you that letter, Jack, and Bob said he'd see it went on the next train. He went off to get the men in the village to search round here just in case Joshua had been taken poorly on his way up. That was last Monday, when the men searched, but there was no trace of him, and on Tuesday they looked again."

"Bob Bainbridge said he'd better tell his inspector in Settle, and the next day he came up in his motor car with another man and they asked all the same questions all over again. You see we haven't many relations at all, there's just you, Jack, and cousin May over in Morecambe, and he wouldn't have gone there - he can't stand her.", she paused for a second and Jack waited patiently. He thought it best to let her get the whole tale told before he asked any questions.

"I'm sick with worry, Jack. I've just had to sit here and wait and wonder and it's getting me down." She reached down and stroked the white bull terrier sitting at her feet, "you've been me only comfort, haven't you lass? She's a lovely girl."

The old dog looked up and dutifully twitched its tail.

"You can leave it all to me now, Aunty." Jack said quietly. "I'm going down to the village in a minute to find out the latest news and see what they're doing."

"Thanks for coming, Jack. I feel better now you're here. It's nice to have some family about at times like this. I'll have some supper ready for you when you get back."

Jack squeezed his aunt's hand affectionately, collected Ruth's suitcase from the hall and headed down to the village.

Jack had spent much of his youth here on the farm with his uncle and aunt after his parents had died. He knew all the best places for birds' nests, where the foxes had their den and the downwind vantage point from which to observe the badgers on the summer evenings. He paused at the gate and looked up the track away from the village. If you followed this path alongside the stream it led eventually into a narrow ravine, dark and foreboding, permanently in shadow and hemmed in by sheer limestone cliffs. Devils' Gill it was called, a place shunned by most of the locals and traditionally feared by the children because of the many bizarre tales of trolls and evil spirits said to live in the caves and haunt its shadowy corners.

Certainly you felt less than welcome when you left the sunshine and entered the narrow passage through the cliffs, and it was always with some relief that you climbed up the stairway of boulders at the far end and came out onto the open fell. Then past Bar Pot, Flood Entrance and on to Gaping Gill and the slopes up to Little Ingleborough and eventually on to the summit of Ingleborough itself; it was an area which had completely captivated the young Warrendale, and its exploration had occupied much of his youthful spare time.

Jack reluctantly brought his mind back to his present problems. His eyes roved from side to side looking for any sign of his uncle. Stupid, he thought. The police and search parties will have gone over this ground meticulously already. Nevertheless his keen eyes continued to scan the fellside all the way to the village.

Jack's first call was at The Old Crown, a pleasant old-established residential hotel overlooking the beck in the main street. To tell the truth he was getting a bit fed up of lugging Ruth's case everywhere, and he thought if he could get rid of it at the hotel it would leave his hands free, as it were, to get on with the more pressing task of finding his uncle.

Jack pushed through the swing door and the clerk behind the reception desk looked up, his face automatically registering his guest-greeting welcome.

"Is a Miss Ruth Lancaster staying here, please?" Jack enquired politely.

"I'll just check for you, sir." The suave young man flicked deftly through the hotel register and then looked up. "She's not in at the moment, sir, but we do have a booking from the 6th". He glanced at the desk calendar, "that's tomorrow," he added.

"Oh, I see," Jack muttered. "I have a suitcase for her. She asked me to deliver it here for her. What room will she be in? Can you tell me?"

"Certainly, sir." He glanced down at the register, "Miss Lancaster will be in Room 25. I'll make certain the suitcase is delivered to her room as soon as she arrives."

Jack was about to hand it over the counter when a vague uneasiness came over him. To this day he has never been able to adequately explain why he didn't leave the case, but he found himself muttering, "No, it's all right, I need to see Miss Lancaster myself so I'll deliver to her it personally tomorrow." Jack was vaguely aware of a newspaper rustling behind him in the reception lounge.

"As you wish, sir," the clerk said, failing completely to keep the condescension out of his voice.

Jack picked up the case and turned to leave and, as he did so, noticed for the first time a gentleman sitting in a wicker basket-chair by the window. His head and shoulders were obscured by the opened newspaper but there was something remarkably familiar about the posture of the man. Jack, however, didn't dwell on it, he was far too interested in getting out of the hotel. He felt he'd made a bit of a fool of himself and he wasn't too keen on these pseudo-classy hotels and their snotty little receptionists. He quite liked a pint in the public bar at the other end of the building but this was the first time he'd ever been in the hotel and he'd not particularly enjoyed the experience.

Still carrying the suitcase he called in at the public bar but the barman wasn't able to tell him anything that he didn't already know. However, that didn't stop him repeating the whole story again and Jack was unable to get away until the, now very well-practised, tale was concluded. And not only the tale but all the conjectures, all the possibilities, the probabilities, and the consensual opinion of the expert analysts in the tap room as well. Jack wished he'd never come in now and he wouldn't have got out so easily either if another customer hadn't arrived just then and momentarily distracted the barman. Jack seized the opportunity gratefully, muttered his thanks and was out of the door in a flash.

More or less the same thing happened down at the Flying Dutchman opposite the railway station. He ordered a pint of bitter and sat in the tap-room with two or three of the regulars. They expressed their sadness at Joss's disappearance; he was a popular character in the village, as well as a good customer at the pubs. However no one was able to add anything to the information Jack had already collected. He was feeling a bit dispirited about this as he left the pub and headed back to the village. Things hadn't quite worked out as he'd hoped. He was none the wiser about his uncle, he hadn't spotted any clues that the police had unaccountably missed like they always did in the Sherlock Holmes stories he'd read, and the hoped-for reunion with Ruth hadn't occurred; in fact, nothing had happened.

He decided to call at Constable Bainbridge's house on the way through the village just to let him know that he was now in the area. The constable lived in one of the small terraced cottages in the main street overlooking the beck, but on the opposite side to The Old Crown. Bob Bainbridge was a large red-faced man, possibly nearing retirement age now, Jack guessed; he'd certainly been here as long as Jack could remember. He was pleased to see Jack and warmly welcomed him into his cosy living room.

"Come in lad, it's grand to see you. How's your aunty going on? She'll feel a lot better now you're here, I'll warrant."

Jack assured the constable that his aunt was coping all right though naturally very worried.

"Aye, she will be. We've notified them down at the station in Settle to keep a look out for him in case he's had a memory loss, or owt like that, you know, and perhaps wandered off in that direction. It sometimes happens, you

---

know. Anyway, lad, we're doing everything we can to find him. I've known Joss for nigh on thirty years, he's a good man."

As the constable was talking Jack glanced out of the window and across the beck to the front door of the hotel. A movement had caught his eye, a man with a folded newspaper under his arm had just left the hotel. Jack's idle gaze suddenly became intently focussed on the dark suited figure of a clergyman. Unless he was very much mistaken it was the same parson he'd seen on the London train the day before. The policeman noticed Jack's interest and turned to look out of the window.

"That's Mr. Bergman, he's a clergyman, from London. He comes up here for a few days holiday quite regularly. He seems to like walking and bird watching, at least I've seen him in his boots with his binoculars. He came in yesterday, always stays at the Crown. I spoke to him this morning in the square, a real gentleman. I think he comes from Holland, at least that's what the locals say."

"We travelled up on the same train yesterday," said Jack. It's just a remarkable coincidence that we should be coming to the same place."

Jack withheld the information that the parson had left the train at the same time as Ruth, but since he'd not mentioned Ruth either he felt it would complicate things too much to start now. Nor did he quite agree with the constable's assessment of the parson's character. Jack still remembered the supercilious look he'd got when he'd first boarded the train at King's Cross.

Jack eventually took his leave of the constable, promising to look in again on the following day. He headed straight up the main street in the direction of his uncle's farm; he was well aware that he was being watched by a clerical eye from the other side of the stream. He strode out purposefully up the road past the church, apparently completely unaware of the other man's presence. However, once in the woods he left the track at one of the bends and scrambled quickly up the slope to look back down the path. Sure enough, as he'd suspected, the single figure of a man in dark clothing was following Jack's route up the valley. He was in no doubt who the man was.

40

As soon as Jack opened the farmhouse door the delicious aroma of home-made meat and potato pie, his aunt's speciality, assailed his nostrils. God, it's great to be back, he thought as he relished the warm, comforting atmosphere of the place. His aunt was standing by the kitchen table in her flour-stained pinny, her sleeves rolled up and an old pair of oven gloves linking her arms together like handcuffs.

"Ar, you're back then, Jack. Dinner's on but it won't be ready for a bit yet. How did you get on today?"

It didn't take him long to tell her the little he had found out but she was heartened by the information that the police had extended their search and were still very involved.

While his aunt was getting the meal ready Jack nipped upstairs, ostensibly to get washed and changed, but really to see if that Bergman fellow came up the track as far as the farm. The bedroom window overlooked the gate where the valley path met the farm-track and Jack looked out over the familiar scene, the stream in the valley bottom and the steep green fellside rising up to the bleak open moor above. His eyes followed the line of the white limestone walls which sectionalised the lower pastures, he noted and attempted to count the sheep grazing in the evening sunshine.

The best view in the world, he thought to himself. Well at least, the best I've seen for a long time, he added as a rider. His attention was distracted by the appearance some minutes later of the expected, and now familiar, figure of Pastor Bergman, or whatever they called him, striding briskly along the path. Jack instinctively drew back from the window and observed the clergyman through the side of the curtain. Bergman paused at the gate, looked keenly at the farmhouse for a long minute, and then turned, and this surprised Jack quite considerably, walked up the path towards Devil's Gill. He strode out purposefully, Jack noticed, with a methodical pace as though he was not just out for an evening stroll, but had a pre-determined destination in mind. Jack breathed out in relief when Bergman disappeared from view, until then he hadn't realised he'd been holding his breath.

What am I worried about? he thought, angry with himself. I don't give a damn what he thinks, or does, for that matter. But he had to admit to himself that there was something sinister about the man, a vague uneasiness settled on Jack whenever he was around.

Jack went downstairs again and chatted to his aunt in the kitchen as he put on his working boots, "By the way, Aunt Dorcas, that young lady I was telling you about isn't coming up until tomorrow, so I've brought the suitcase back. I didn't feel like leaving it in the village, it's in the hallway."

"You did right, lad. There's some peculiar folk about in yon village just lately." She nodded her head knowingly to emphasise the point.

"How do you mean, Auntie?" Jack asked quickly, unable to conceal his immediate interest.

"Well, the other week, Mrs.Thornton, that's her who does the church during the week, and knows everything that goes on round here told me," and here her voice dropped to a whisper so that Jack had to lean forward to catch her words, " .. that smugglers are operating in this area."

Jack exploded in involuntary laughter, "Nay, come on Auntie, there are no smugglers round here. There's nowt to smuggle for one thing, and nowhere to smuggle it to for another."

"Well, that's what I thought, Jack, but I didn't like to say, she being such a church-goer and all. She said she'd seen 'em two or three times, very late at night, or early in the morning, always wearing dark clothes and carrying small boxes and, she told me", his aunt lowered her voice again, just as Mrs Thornton had done, Jack guessed, "they moved without making a sound".

Jack couldn't quite stifle his scornful laugh but he didn't want to upset his aunt because she was obviously only repeating the story that Mrs Thornton had told her.

"Do you remember when she told us there was a ghost in the churchyard? ", Jack reminded his Aunt. "I was still at school then and I used to be terrified of passing that church after dark. I still get a funny feeling about it even now."

"Nay, surely not," his Aunt smiled. "I must admit she's a bit of a queer stick is Mary Thornton. I think it's with living on her own all this time."

Jack nodded his agreement, "Aye, probably so. Look Auntie I'm just going to have a look at the sheep in that field across the valley. How long have I got before supper?"

His Aunt turned round and opened the oven door, "I should think it'll be ready in about half an hour or so, so think on, don't go too far, Jack."

Jack took his jacket off the peg in the hallway and left the farm. "Come on lass, are you coming with me?" he called out to the bull terrier. The rapid scurrying of paws on the lino gave him his answer and the pair of them set off down the farm track together. The evening sunlight on the far side of the valley was diminishing by the minute as the shadows crept inexorably up the fellside, but it was still warm and the air was particularly still; they'd been very lucky with the weather just recently.

The steep sided valleys of the area had various terraced levels along which either footpaths or bridleways had been established over the years. It was to one of these higher contoured tracks that Jack was making for this particular evening. He knew the route well and he also knew he could be there and back in about thirty minutes. Also from the vantage point he had in mind he knew he would have a good view up the valley past the crags at the head of the Gill and onto the open moor. He was gasping for breath and his heart was racing when he reached the track, "Whew, I'm well out of condition, what about you lass?" The dog seemed to have coped quite comfortably with such an ascent and was ferreting about near some rabbit holes.

Jack leaned on the dry-stone wall and looked back across the valley at his uncle's farm, an idyllic picture, the smoke from the chimney rising vertically in the still air. The sun was low in the sky but visibility was still quite good and he could pick out all the familiar landmarks. His eyes roved about for a while until his attention became riveted on two specks way up the valley. Two people, standing he guessed, somewhere in the region of the Gaping Gill cave system, that famous and dramatic cleft in the surface of the moor.

Jack was fairly familiar with the underground system; he'd been down Bar Pot on a couple of occasions with the Caving Club from Settle. He remembered standing in awe at the bottom of the great cathedral-like chamber in Gaping Gill, staring up at the silvery wisp of stream water entering through a tiny hole in the roof of the cavern hundreds of feet above his head. As he watched and reminisced Jack noticed that the figures were on the move, heading down the valley in his direction. He was not able to identify them from this distance, they might just be a pair of ramblers returning from a day in the hills.

He'd seen enough for the evening and he was feeling decidedly hungry now so he went bounding down the hillside, the dog leaping about him as he descended. He was back at the farm in less than ten minutes, but the uphill pull to the house had really taken it out of him and he was glad to sit on the doorstep for a minute or two to recover. Still, he was grateful for the fresh air and the exercise. He knew it would be at least another twenty minutes before the walkers he'd seen earlier appeared on the lane below the farm; he would be interested to see if Bergman was one of them.

The meal his aunt had prepared was the one he'd always dreamed about when doing his own cooking in his London flat. The first course was the statutory Yorkshire pudding, as big as a flat cap and filled with a rich brown onion gravy; a meal in itself. Jack quickly despatched this delicacy and then loosened his belt to tackle the main course, the aforementioned meat and potato pie, accompanied by liberal helpings of garden peas and carrots.

She's a grand cook is Aunt Dorcas, thought Jack, something of a connoisseur himself on the eating side of the culinary world, as he sat back in his chair.

"Thanks, Auntie, that was lovely. I'd nearly forgotten what a brilliant cook you are."

"You're welcome, lad, I'm sure," his aunt replied. "I'm glad to be able to cook for someone. I've been terribly lonely just lately." She moved her chair closer to the fire. "Come and have your tea nearer the fire. There's a piece of spice cake and some cheese to finish off with; I didn't bother making a pudding tonight."

"Right, thanks very much, it's just as well really, I don't think I could have managed anymore just at the moment." Jack picked up his pot of tea and moved casually over to the window and looked down the valley. He'd kept an eye on the time during supper and he was expecting to see someone coming down the track any time now. He passed the time chatting to his aunt about the weather, the livestock on the farm and in the pastures, and the general life and notable events in the village, although these tended to be very much parochial affairs. The main one by far being the annual village fete which had been held about a fortnight ago, and according to his aunt had been a huge success this year. She'd obviously thoroughly enjoyed it and Jack was tempted to believe that this was probably because it was the only social engagement she'd been able to manage this year, although, of course, he never mentioned this.

It was perhaps ten minutes later that a single figure appeared, male, obviously, and walking swiftly down the track in the direction of the village. Bergman, Jack decided, as the walker reached the gate, but was he one of the two Jack had seen up the hillside? Or were there still two others to come down? Jack stayed at the window, his hands wrapped round his pint mug, until the light outside began to fade. There had been no other sign of travellers since Bergman so Jack drew the curtains and joined his Aunt by the hearth. They sat in the glow of the firelight for some time, both staring semi-hypnotised into the glowing coals, each forming different images and dreaming different dreams. Jack wondered afterwards what his aunt saw in the coals and whether, like him, she dreamed of what might be in the future, or whether people of her age simply relived memories. He didn't feel it was something he could ask in the present situation but he decided himself, in an unusual spell of philosophical thought, that the state of old age has been reached when a person spends more time thinking about the past than he or she does dreaming and planning for the future. Jack's profound thoughts were distracted by his aunt moving in her chair as though to get up.

"What is it, Auntie? Do you want me to get you something?" volunteered Jack.

"No, it's all right, love. I was just going to light up and do the washing up."

"You stay there, Auntie. I'll see to the light and I'll put the kettle on for the washing up." Jack lifted the paraffin lamp down from the shelf; it took him a minute or two to work out just how to get it going, even though he'd regularly lit it in the past. When the paraffin eventually vaporised and the lamp was hissing away steadily Jack placed it on the table where it's pale lunar light cast long shadows into the corners of the kitchen. He filled the huge copper kettle and placed it on the hob and swung it over the fire and settled down in his chair again opposite his aunt. He bent down and ran his hand across the hot fur on the dog's back as it lay there, stewed into immobility on the hearthrug.

Jack looked around the kitchen and tried to decide what exactly it was that created such a homely, comfortable and secure atmosphere in the farmhouse kitchen. He decided that it was the combination of factors, the whole being more important then the individual parts, but the builders of old certainly knew what there were doing when they constructed buildings like these. How could people possibly spend all their lives in places like the one he inhabited in London; cold, impersonal, lacking in character. His train of thought was interrupted by the sound of the kettle boiling and he reached over with the poker and gently swung the hob back to the side.

He noticed his aunt had dozed off; she looked very sweet and comfortable with her tartan shawl draped over her knees and her hands clasped on her lap. He quietly got to his feet, lifted the heavy kettle over to the sink and washed up the crockery and the pans, handling each piece carefully to avoid making a sound. When they were all on the draining board he made two cups of cocoa and took them over to the fireside and gently woke his aunt.

"Eeeh, thanks lad. That's very nice of you. What time is it now?"

Jack peered up at the clock on the mantelpiece, "It's just gone nine o'clock," he answered.

"Ah well, it's allus ten minutes fast, is yon. So it'll be nearly nine. I must have dozed off for a minute or two."

They sat together with their mugs of cocoa for another twenty minutes or so and than Jack excused himself on the grounds that he wanted to make an early start in the morning. He lit two smaller paraffin lamps, one for each of them, wished his aunt goodnight and retired to his bedroom.

Comfortable though he was in bed, sleep did not come easily. His mind wandered over the events of the last couple of days; his uncle's disappearance, Ruth Lancaster and her suitcase, Bergman and his trek up the valley, sheep rustlers in the night. Appropriately enough he fell sound asleep whilst considering the latter possibility and knew nothing else until he was awakened by the morning sunlight streaming through the gap in the curtain and making familiar shapes on the bedroom wall.

He smiled to himself as he recognised the Santa Claus figure in the shadow near the door; his mind went straight back to his early schooldays; it was as though it was yesterday. He knew he could lie in bed until the figure reached the corner of the wall before his aunt would start calling from the kitchen to get him up for school. Today, however, he needed no such cajoling, he got himself up, washed and dressed leisurely, and went down to enjoy the substantial farmhouse breakfast his aunt had prepared.

Five

Langham, Yorkshire Dales, 6ᵗʰ July 1939

Jack strode briskly down the lane towards the village that morning enjoying the opportunity for some exercise in the sunshine. He'd decided to leave Ruth's suitcase at the farm as he didn't expect her to arrive until late afternoon and he felt particularly energetic and unencumbered as a result. He paused briefly at the side of the lake, still as a mill-pond this morning, looking for the family of tufted ducks but as yet there was no sign of them today.

His first call that morning was at Constable Bainbridge's cottage in the main street. He was not expecting any news as he'd only been there the previous afternoon so he was pleasantly surprised when the constable came to meet him as he was opening the gate.

"I was just going to bike up to see you," he said cheerfully. "I've just had a telegram."

"Have you found him?" Jack interrupted excitedly.

"Nay, I'm sorry I raised your hopes, lad. It's just that we think we've had a sighting in Settle. Inspector Bannerman's coming over by motor car today to see you about it. He's new to the area, I haven't even met him meself yet."

"Well, at least things are moving a bit," Jack said quietly, trying hard to conceal the disappointment. "I'm just going to wander around a bit this morning and talk to people in the village."

He thanked Bainbridge for the message, crossed the beck on the pack-horse bridge and headed up the other side of the main street towards the church. He was going to call on Mrs.Thornton, his aunt's friend and fount of all village knowledge.

The door of the cottage was answered almost immediately by the small, elderly, sharp-featured lady Jack had remembered from his youth. She actually appeared younger than when he'd last seen her some seven or eight years ago. It was her sharp, bright blue restless eyes, he decided, which gave that impression of youthful curiosity.

"Hello, Mrs.Thornton, do you remember me? I'm Jack Warrendale, Joss and Dorcas's nephew."

"Oh aye, I remember thee. Come in, lad, you'll be looking for your uncle, I'll bet. I heard you was up."

"Aye, I am. I've just come up from London to help out, but nobody seems to know anything round here."

"I told him to be careful the day before he disappeared. I'll tell you, lad, people laugh at me, don't think I don't know, but I know what's going on"

"I didn't realise you'd seen Uncle Joss so recently. Did you just happen to meet, like?"

Mrs Thornton looked at Jack shrewdly before replying, "Joss come here to see me because he was worried about something." She paused for dramatic effect as if she was in the post office queue with a full audience. "He knew I'd know if there was owt untoward going on."

Jack could hardly contain his excitement, he wanted to blurt out, "Go on then, what for God's sake?" Fortunately he restrained himself knowing that infinite patience would be needed in this situation and that this tale, like all her tales, would take a lot of telling.

It transpired that Joss Warrendale had called on Mrs Thornton on the Sunday before he'd disappeared. They'd known each other all their lives, she was careful to point out, and they chatted over a cup of tea and a buttered scone, just a general conversation about the village, the farms and the weather. Then Joss had asked, 'out of the blue' she said, about the smugglers she'd seen during the night. She told him, she said. She'd not been mistaken. Usually about the time of the full moon, three, sometimes four, men moving very quietly through the village towards the main road. They were always dressed in black and some of them were carrying suitcases.

Jack asked her how many times she'd seen these strangers.

"I've seen 'em twice now. I told your uncle, and I told him to be careful as they seemed to come down the lane past his farm. He said he'd watch out for 'em. I asked him why he'd come to me because everybody else thought I was dreaming it, especially that stupid bobby down the road. I reported it to him ages ago, and do you know what he said?"

Jack shook his head, unwilling to hazard a guess and interrupt the flow.

"He said, you're imagining it. Fancy that. Can you believe it? Why should I want to imagine four young men walking the streets at night?" She stared directly into Jack's eyes for an answer. Jack held her gaze but wisely desisted from an incautious reply and simply shook his head slowly in sympathetic disbelief.

"I think they're smugglers, that's what I think," she said with some conviction. Your uncle thought they might be sheep rustlers, 'cos he's lost a few recently, but I told him I could tell the difference between a sheep and a suitcase, and they didn't have no sheep under their arms, they had suitcases."

Jack thanked Mrs Thornton and promised to keep in touch. She's a queer old bird, he thought as he said goodbye and went out into the main street. Interesting though, and I tended to believe what she said about people walking through the village at night.

Jack's next call was at the small general stores run by Mrs. Keighley, another of his aunt's friends. His Uncle Joss was a regular caller here, both for the weekly groceries as well as for his supply of pipe tobacco. Jack just wanted to speak to her about the last time his uncle had called, even though he knew that Constable Bainbridge would have already questioned her.

The shop was exactly has he had remembered it; a quaint Victorian relic. It must have always smelled like this, Jack thought, a dusty, musty, fascinating aggregation of life's necessities. Sacks of potatoes lay open on the floor alongside boxes of vegetables, trays of eggs were stacked at one end of the counter next to a leg of pork and an antiquated bacon-slicer. Only a tiny fraction of the counter was actually visible, the rest being smothered in a multiplicity of commodities, various and diverse. Mrs Keighley appeared from the back room at the sound of the door-bell and headed for her minute space behind the counter.

"Hello, Mrs Keighley."

The elderly shopkeeper peered up at Jack, "Hello, it's Jack, isn't it? Dorcas's Jack from High Top Farm," she said after she'd adjusted her spectacles to focus on his face.

Jack nodded and smiled, "How are you keeping, Mrs Keighley?"

"Ay, I'm right enough Jack, thanks. It's your Dorcas I'm worried about, she'll be glad you're up here with her now. She told me you were probably coming up when I saw her the other day. I think Joss has been working too hard, you know. He nivver stops, he's taking too much on if you ask me, what with the farm to run and Dorcas not being able to get about like she used to. 'It's time you retired' I told him last time I saw him."

Jack seized the opportunity to stop the flow of words and butted in. "When was that, Mrs Keighley? When was the last time you saw him? Can you remember?"

"Aye, course I can. My memory's as sharp as ever it was. I was only saying to Mrs Hill this morning, that's the lady who does for them at the Manor, that I can remember when Queen Victoria died. It was five years after me and Bill got married. We took this shop a couple of years after that and we've been here ever since. Mind you, Bill came from the village, his father had the smithy over the road, but I came from Settle. I met him at the church dance one Christmas. Eeh, those were the days, eh?"

As she paused to savour the good old days, Jack took his chance to get a word in again, "When did you say you saw Uncle Joss, Mrs Keighley? Was it this week?"

"What? Who?" she looked at Jack and reluctantly clawed her way to the present. "Oh, yes, now let's see, when did he come in? Ah, I remember."

Jack brightened, at last, at long last, he thought.

"He bought half a dozen eggs, a stone of potatoes, King Edwards, I think. Yes, definitely, because it was a new sack, they'd just been delivered by that chap from Bentham, and your Joss had to open it for me. And what else was it he got? Oh, I know. I told you I had a good memory, a packet of sugar and two ounce of tobacco." She looked at Jack triumphantly as she finished the shopping list. He smiled, inwardly squirming with frustration. Thank God I'm not in the police force and have to do this for a living, he thought. Aloud he said, "so it must have been Saturday then when he came in."

"Aye, it could well have been. You see I usually do a bit of washing early on, on a Saturday." She gazed at the ceiling for a second in silent reflection as if mentally checking the washing line.

Jack butted in, "Well thanks for your help, Mrs Keighley. I've got to get down to the station to meet the eleven o'clock train." He glanced at his watch to add urgency to his departure and backed hurriedly out of the shop before she could start another monologue. He stumbled out into the bright morning light momentarily dazzled after the gloomy interior of the shop.

"I can do without all that," he muttered to himself, "I could have been there all day."

He had not intended to go down to the railway station that morning but once the idea had come into his head it refused to leave. Ruth probably wouldn't be on the early train anyway he reasoned, but as The Flying Dutchman was very near the station and as he needed to speak to the landlord there he might as well go down and just check on the early train at the same time.

The station platform was deserted when he got there. He nodded to the booking clerk and had a few words with him and then wandered up and down the platform for a while. It was a pleasant rural station and Harold Winterburn, the stationmaster, was very proud of his responsibility. His troughs of flowers and magnificent hanging baskets were a credit to him and were the pride of the London, Midland and Scottish. The painted railings and whitewashed rockery stones were a throwback to his years as a sergeant in the Duke of Wellington's Regiment during the Great War. If it stands still paint it, if it moves salute it, being the old army adage.

A few women from the village arrived after a couple of minutes, baskets on their arms, chatting animatedly amongst themselves. Jack observed them from the far end of the platform. He didn't know them individually, but he knew they were going for an afternoon's shopping in Bentham, the next reasonably-sized community up the line. They'd be coming back on the five-thirty, he guessed.

Now that he was actually here waiting for the train, Jack was not too sure how to deal with the situation if Ruth was actually on it. She had invaded his mind so completely over the last few days and he had often daydreamed of running up to her on the platform, embracing her and then strolling up to the village together arm in arm. Now the moment which he'd been looking forward to had come and he was full of self-doubt; suppose she didn't remember him? What if she didn't even recognise him? They were only together for such a short time and perhaps he'd not made as much an impression on her as she had on him. God, this is awful, he thought.

He could see the smoke from the engine down the line, followed some minutes later, by the familiar noise of the straining engine as it laboured up the slight incline towards the station. Jack drew back alongside one of the ornately carved pillars at the far end of the platform to observe the train's arrival from a distance. If Ruth got off the train and seemed to be looking around for him then he would go and meet her, if not? Well he hadn't really worked that one out yet. He was aware that his heart was beating at an incredible speed as he wiped his palms on the sides of his trousers and smoothed his hair down. It was whilst he was engaged in this self-conscious grooming that he became aware of the now too-familiar figure of the ubiquitous vicar, Bergman. Jack was annoyed. What the devil was he doing here? Everywhere I go that bloody chap seems to be there as well. He was glad now that he'd kept in the background as Bergman hadn't appeared to have noticed him, so intently was his gaze fixed on the incoming train.

With a grinding of metal and in a cloud of escaping steam the locomotive drew alongside the platform. Jack was momentarily engulfed in the billowing cloud as the engine stopped just opposite his position. Doors opened all the way along the four carriages and people spilled out onto the platform. Jack stood on tiptoe to see over the heads of people leaving the nearest compartment.

There she was! Oh, God there she was, two carriages down.

Jack instinctively moved towards her, and then stopped in acute embarrassment. She was not alone. A tall, fair-haired man, carrying a suitcase in his left hand was walking beside her, and it looked as though another man just behind them was also in the same party. They'd formed a sort of distinctive little unit, Jack thought, as they headed purposefully towards the exit. Aware now that he was in an exposed position and that the vicar was watching him he rapidly collected his wits and went to intercept the group.

"Ruth!" he called as he got nearer, "Hello, again. Do you remember me? Jack Warrendale, we met on the train. I brought your suitcase up."

She half-smiled; scarcely the ecstatic welcome he'd hoped for, polite and formal more aptly fitted it. There was, Jack thought, a certain worried look in her eyes; he guessed too that she'd not been entirely surprised by his presence, but it was the subdued tone of her voice that really bothered him.

"Of course, Jack. It was good of you to go to all that trouble." She smiled what Jack could only later recall as a somewhat bleak attempt at warmth. "Here's your case, by the way." She turned her head to the man on her left, "This is my brother, Ernest, and this is his friend, Henry. They've come up to the Dales for a walking weekend."

Jack shook hands with Ernest, a cold, unfriendly hand, he thought, and he didn't much like the steady, almost hostile look in the man's eyes. The other man just gave a curt nod in Jack's direction and immediately looked away.

"It was good of you to meet the train, Jack," Ruth said, drawing Jack's attention away from the men. "Have you got my suitcase with you, by any chance?"

Jack felt even more uncomfortable at this remark and he blurted out, "No, I'm sorry, it's up in the village. I'll bring it over to the hotel straight away." He was aware of the men exchanging glances, and looking into Ruth's eyes he sensed a warning. He was still thinking about this when he heard her saying, "Thanks very much then, that's very kind of you. We'll get a taxi up to the hotel, can we offer you a lift anywhere?"

"No, no thank you," mumbled Jack. "I er I've somewhere else to go first." He desperately needed some time on his own to try and sort things out in his mind.

"Right, well I'll see you later, then. Goodbye for now", Ruth remarked briskly and strode out through the ticket barrier and disappeared through the exit closely followed by the two men.

To say that Jack was rather bewildered would have been a gross understatement. He flopped down on the nearest bench, his mind overflowing with conflicting thoughts. He hardly noticed as the guard's whistle blew and the engine groaned in its exertions as it took up the load and slowly dragged its length up the line.

Left alone with his thoughts on the now peaceful and deserted platform Jack was able to come to some conclusions. Ruth was not with those two men voluntarily, that much was certain. Ernest was certainly not her brother; her parents would have mentioned that to him earlier, and the tension in the group was just too palpable for it to be any kind of friendly trip. No, there was something going on which worried him a great deal, and somehow he felt that whatever he did now could seriously affect the outcome, and that could mean problems for Ruth. And what about the parson? As far as Jack knew he hadn't come to see anybody off or to meet anyone. Jack had forgotten about him until now. He glanced around the station. Well, he wasn't anywhere in sight, thank God. He would have felt even more of a fool if he'd been observed sitting here on the bench looking absolutely dumbstruck.

Jack made his way onto the station forecourt; there was no one around but he could see some of the passengers making their way up the lane towards the village. Of Ruth's party, or the vicar, there was no sign.

Best thing to do, Jack decided, was to go and have a quiet pint and work out a logical and positive course of action. Otherwise he might be rushed into making hasty and possibly disastrous decisions. With these thoughts in mind Jack went into the tap room of the Flying Dutchman, ordered a pint of bitter and settled down at a corner table, still confused, but at least prepared to approach the problem in a more rational state of mind.

Six

Beckley, Lancashire Fells, 6th July 1939

Beck Fell House is a typical Dales farmhouse; built of local gritstone it presents a grey, weather-beaten frontage to anyone walking up the winding road from the village of Beckley, a couple of miles away in the valley bottom. The back of the farm is sheltered from the elements to some extent by a steep gradient of fellside which leads eventually to the summit of Gragareth, some two thousand feet above sea level.

The Gragareth ridge is one of many parallel ridges in the area, each stretching out like the fingers of an extended hand lying on the plain to the west. In the dales between the ridges the U-shaped valleys with their steep sided fells, lined in many places with exposed limestone escarpments, provide a picturesque habitat for the few householders and large numbers of sheep in the area.

Samuel and Hannah Craven had farmed Beck Fell for over twenty-five years. They'd brought up two children there, not an easy task when the nearest hamlet was two miles down the valley, and the nearest neighbour half a mile away. Often in the severe winters they'd been snowed in for weeks on end and the only possible social contact, a visit to their neighbours, entailed a long and arduous struggle through the snowdrifts. It was a hard life in a frequently hostile environment, but there were many advantages; the dramatic beauty of the surroundings, the variety of the changing seasons and a healthy and natural way of life. Sam Craven had been born into the farming life and knew little other than the struggle for the survival of his family and his livestock.

His wife, Hannah, was also of farming stock; she was a sturdy robust woman in her early fifties with the weather-beaten face of one used to the vagaries of the English climate and the outdoor life. Increasingly, in recent years, they had discussed the question of retirement and the possibility of selling up and buying a bungalow in Morecambe. The children had moved away, the boy to college in Leeds and the girl to get married and a home in Skipton; neither had showed much sign of being interested in farming as a career and Sam had not pushed them in this respect.

Sheep farming did, however, have some advantages. Many a time Samuel, as his wife called him, and Hannah had stood on the summit ridge of Gragareth and just exulted in the joy of living in such a glorious place, they had gazed at the sands of Morecambe Bay to the west shimmering silver in the light of the setting sun on a warm summer's evening, or at the peaks of the Lake District mountains to the northwest etched clearly in the olive-green light of the evening sky.

One evening at the beginning of July, shortly after the sun had gone down, but while the ruddy glow still lit the upper slopes of the fellside opposite, Sam and Hannah were disturbed by the menacing growl of Bella, their border collie. Bella had been with them since she was a pup, she'd come from Sam's cousin, or possibly his second cousin? Everyone around here was related somehow, animals as well as people. Bella was an excellent guard dog and extremely well-trained and obedient. Sam, in fact, always maintained that he couldn't manage his work without her. On this particular evening she was watching the door intently and growling in her throat. Sam and Hannah were not unduly worried at this as she would bark at friends, in the first instance, as well as strangers. Also, particularly in the summer months, they often got ramblers returning from a long day in the hills coming down the track alongside the farm. Sometimes they would call at the farm, it being the first sign of habitation they came across, just to reassure themselves they were on the right track. They always got a pleasant welcome from the homely couple who were grateful for the opportunity for a chat and news from different parts of the county.

After some minutes of the continuous growling Sam muttered, "Enough, girl". He rose to his feet and went to the door with the dog at his heels. "Good girl, what have you heard, then?" He opened the upper part of the door and looked out into the twilight. "Look at this gorgeous sky, love," he called over his shoulder to his wife. Hannah joined him at the door and they stood leaning on the lower part of the stable door looking at the rosy hues in the western sky which, as they watched, mellowed to mauve and olive over the hills to the north as the night closed in on the valley.

"It must have been a fox, lass," Sam said to the dog bending down to stroke her head. "You're a lovely lass, aren't you?" The dog wagged her tail in enthusiastic agreement. "There's nobody on the road, you can see clear as daylight down there."

After a minute or two Hannah shivered and went inside to make a cup of cocoa for their supper. They usually retired to bed quite early, sometimes they listened to the radio in the evening. They particularly enjoyed "Monday Night at Eight," it helped keep them in touch with the outside world, Hannah used to say.

They slept as soundly as usual that night and neither they nor Bella were aware of the dark shape that banked in the sky above their heads and passed over the cairns behind the farmhouse and disappeared over the ridge towards Kingsdale.

Next morning dawned bright and clear and Sam was out of the farm and striding up the fellside with Bella at his heels well before 7.30. He wanted to check on some of his sheep up by the boundary wall on the ridge. He paused briefly at the three cairns and looked down on his farmhouse. His heart always warmed when he saw it from this angle; it looked so cosy and snug, as indeed it was. Already smoke was curling up from the chimney as Hannah lit the fire to prepare breakfast. He turned to climb farther up the hillside when his attention was drawn to Bella who was chewing something in amongst a circle of rocks.

"Come on, lass, leave it!" It'd be a crust of bread or a mouldy piece of sandwich she'd found; she loved these surprise delicacies in the same way a gourmet would on discovering a rich vein of truffles at the bottom of his garden. Sam walked over to her, sure enough she was wolfing down half a sandwich which, Sam noticed with surprise, was relatively fresh compared with the usual fare. "Leave, I said," rather more sharply this time and he bent down to grab her collar and pull her away. It was then that he noticed the edge of a black box protruding from beneath a pile of flat stones. "Bloody hell," he muttered as cleared some of the stones away. "Who the hell's dragged this bloody thing all the way up here?" It looked like some kind of lead battery, but it was much bigger than the usual car battery. And why? he wondered. "Good girl," he added without thinking, and the dog, without questioning the sudden change of mood, promptly finished the rest of the sandwich and foraged around for more of the same.

Sam looked around warily, his suspicions well aroused now. A lead battery at that height defied rational explanation. His first thoughts were of cavers, that new-fangled sport which sent people underground, but he'd seen a few of them around already and they had lights on their helmets, and smelly carbide lamps at that. It could only be to provide some light up here, he reasoned, as he carefully replaced the stones on the battery. And that in itself, was highly suspicious. He'd best keep an eye on things around here, he thought. He'd I lost enough sheep through natural causes as it was!

He continued up the hillside, in a different mood now, a feeling he didn't like had come over him. The peace of the morning had been disturbed, something he didn't understand, something that didn't fit in with his world was going on, and in his territory too, and he should know about it. The thoughts tumbled about in his mind as he strode over the close-cropped grass and up to the wall that ran along the ridge. Looking down into the next valley, Kingsdale, he could see a few sheep on the nearside slope, they could be his, part of the wall was down. One silly bugger would jump over and knock stones off the top and then the rest would follow, before you know where you are you've got a big repair job on your hands.

These working thoughts forced Sam's earlier worries out of his mind as he followed the wall along the ridge. Ingleborough stood out stark and dramatic in the morning sunlight and the rising ground mist in Kingsdale was clearing rapidly as the day got warmer. The farm at Braida Garth, across the valley was just becoming visible through the haze.

It was a fairly steep drop down to the Turbary Road, that ancient drove road which followed a shelf-like route above the dale. Sam took it very slowly, his knees which had given him great service all his life, now complained rather painfully on steep descents.

On one of his frequent pauses as he descended the slope his keen eyes spotted a group of people near one of the cave entrances. He didn"t give it a great deal of thought as you sometimes got cavers up in these parts nowadays. Weird sort of folk, scruffy buggers, half-men half-beast, floundering about underground in pitch darkness up to their necks in mud on a glorious summer's day. As far as he could tell from this distance they seemed to be around the Rowten Pot system.

Sam made his way down steadily down the slope and quickened his pace once he reached the level road. He had not come across any of his sheep down here at all and he'd decided to head along the track for a while in the direction of Yordas Cave before going up the fellside again. "Time for a smoke and a rest, old girl", he called to the dog. She came up fussily, tail wagging, but her lip curled and she gave him a reproving look when she caught the scent of Sam's tobacco. He leaned on one gate and stared across the open ground in the direction of the cavers, they were still there; three of them, and he knew now that they were at the entrance to Rowten Cave.

"Come on, lass", he said, as he headed across the rough grass towards them. He'd now forgotten his earlier misgivings and was once again full of the joy of the morning, and a friendly chat and a shared moment with strangers somehow appealed to him. He waved a greeting to the men as he got nearer and was surprised to observe what appeared to be quite frenzied activity on their part. When Sam reached the rocky outcrop above the cave entrance there was only one of the men standing there, a single knapsack at his feet. Of the others there was no sign.

"Hello, there. Grand morning!" Sam called out cheerily.

"Hello" the man replied. He was wearing heavy walking boots, Sam noted, but he didn't look much like a caver; he wasn't dirty enough for a start.

"Come here, lass. Enough!", he admonished, as Bella barked and began to growl at the stranger. "Are you staying up here long?" Sam enquired.

"No, we came up this morning to look at the caves, going back tonight."

Sounds a bit foreign to me, an offcumden thought Sam, Irish or something like that. Aloud he said," I'm just having a wander around checking the sheep; some have strayed down this side, I think."

"Where do you live? Near here?" the stranger asked.

"Over that ridge, in the next valley," he pointed up the slope towards Gragareth. "Well I suppose I'd better be getting on, good day to you."

"Goodbye", the man answered, without any great enthusiasm, Sam felt. That conversation had been a bit of a dampener, he thought, and unnatural too. He got the uneasy impression that the other men were only just out of sight in the cave, listening to every word and waiting for him to go.

It must have been nearly an hour later that Sam regained the ridge. He sat down for a breather and studied the land below. He soon made out three tiny figures around the cave mouth; he could tell something was up by the amount of arm waving and pointing that was going on. He would have been even more intrigued if he'd realised that one of the men was his old pal and neighbour, Joss Warrendale.

Two of the men had dragged something heavy out of the cave and were busy erecting a long pole over it. Sam was completely absorbed in watching the operation down below, he had at first thought it was some kind of extending ladder for potholing; now it dawned on him, and he cursed himself for being so slow-witted. It was a wireless antennae. They were rigging up a transmitter. Of course, it all tied up now, the battery down near his place, the wireless set on this side, this lot were up to no good.

He'd seen enough now and his clear duty was to report his suspicions to the authorities, whose representative, in his case, was Police Constable Jim Birkwith down in Beckley village.

"Shut up, girl !", he said as Bella growled menacingly, "We've got work to do, and no time to lose." He struggled to his feet, using the dog's collar to help pull himself up, turned up the slope and found himself looking straight into the barrel of a large pistol.

"What the bloody?", he exclaimed automatically.

"Shut up and listen", the voice was curt, commanding and distinctly hostile. The speaker was a well-built young man with fair hair and a ruddy outdoor complexion. He was dressed in a plain dark green military type of tunic, matching trousers, heavy boots and a green forage cap. He looked every inch a soldier, Sam thought, except for the lack of badges.

"What is this?", Sam retorted angrily, trying at the same time to quieten the dog. "I farm this land, and what the hell are you doing here?"

"No more questions. Come this way", he indicated up the slope with the gun and his manner didn't seem to afford the opportunity for reasoned discussion. Sam was more amazed than frightened. He'd worked this fellside man and boy for nigh on thirty years and nothing even remotely like this had happened to him before. He preceded the man to the boundary wall clasping Bella by her collar and trying to work out what to do.

At the wall they were met by two other man, similarly dressed. Sam was ordered to climb over the wall and as he did so he noticed a wireless set by the feet of one of the men. The man with the gun motioned Sam to sit down and then sat opposite him with the pistol trained directly at Sam's stomach. The signaller dragged the wireless set some distance away and pulled out a telescopic metal aerial. Sam had seen field wireless sets before when he served with the King's Own Yorkshire Light Infantry during the Great War, but nothing as sophisticated as this. He was more than a little intrigued by it all. The wireless operator had put on a headset and had switched on the set. Sam was too far away to hear what was being said but he could tell immediately they were not speaking English, it sounded like German, he thought. He guessed that the party down by the cave were being told about his capture. The operator was listening intently and nodding his head in agreement with what was being said. Sam assumed the man was speaking to someone of superior rank as he appeared to be receiving certain orders, at the conclusion of which he jerked his head smartly in a deferential bow, as if he was actually face to face with his commanding officer.

The operator dismantled the headphones, retracted the aerial and packed them, with the wireless set, into a large framed backpack. It was very heavy and the other man had to help lift it on to the operator's back and adjust the harness for him.

"Come. We go now to your house," the first man informed Sam curtly, and pointed the way with the pistol.

"That's very hospitable of you," grunted Sam. "Will there be anymore of you?"

"You have seen enough and know too much already. We have to change plans accordingly," the man with the gun informed him.

"May I ask what your plans are then?" queried Sam quietly.

"No more questions. You will not be hurt if you do as you are told." was the short reply.

They remained silent from then on as they made their way to the three cairns overlooking the farmhouse. A thin plume of grey smoke was rising vertically out of the chimney pot and Sam looked down at the tranquil, and very familiar scene, with, for the first time, a touch of fear in his heart. He hoped Hannah was all right, or that she wouldn't panic or do anything stupid.

It all seemed so ridiculous and unreal; he could even see a pair of his own socks hanging on the washing line.

The wireless operator removed the knapsack at the cairns and concealed it near the battery Sam had discovered earlier in the day.

"Right, down to the house. How many people there?"

Sam saw no reason to be evasive, "Just my wife," he said. "That's all."

The wireless operator led the way down the hillside, followed by Sam and the two other men. At the back door Sam was pushed in first, the barrel of the pistol prodding his back.

"Hello, love", he called brightly. "It's only me."

His wife was standing at the table cutting up some vegetables as they entered the kitchen. She half turned, "Hello, love, I expected you ages ago....", her voice trailed off as she became aware of the other people behind him.

"I've brought some people down with me, Hannah," he said in an attempt to ease the situation.

She smiled, "Oh, come in then, you're welc...," she broke off abruptly when she saw the gun in the man's hand. She gasped, her face suddenly ashen with shock, "Samuel?" she cried. "What is it, what do they want?" She was beginning to panic and Sam moved across to calm her down.

"It's all right, love. They're not going to harm us."

"It is as your husband says," the gunman confirmed. "You will not be hurt. We will not be here long. We have a job to do and when it is done, we will go. Until then everything must appear normal. Do you understand?"

"I suppose so," said Sam, still with his arm around Hannah. "How long will you be staying here? Can you tell us that?"

"Tonight and tomorrow night, then we go," answered the man with the gun.

Sam looked down at Hannah; he could feel she was beginning to relax a little now, "Better get the kettle on then, lass. I could do with a pot o'tea."

Seven

Langham, Yorkshire Dales, 6th July 1939

Jack came out of The Flying Dutchman into the glare of the midday sunshine. He blinked his eyes, he had not realised it was as bright as this when he had gone in; perhaps it was just the contrast between the gloom of the tap room and the outside world. Over a reflective pint of bitter Jack had decided what course of action he should take. He felt sure that Ruth's suitcase held the answers to many questions and he knew he must return it to her today. However, before he did so, he was going to have a look inside and find out why certain people seemed so interested in it.

He was striding up the lane towards the village, heading back to the farm to carry out his resolve, when he heard a motor vehicle coming up behind him. He stepped off the road onto the grass verge to allow it plenty of room to pass. It was a Rover fourteen hp saloon, one of the new ones he noted with interest. However, instead of driving past it drew alongside Jack and stopped. The driver, smartly dressed, in his mid to late thirties, a complete stranger to Jack, leaned across the passenger seat and called out,

"Jack Warrendale?"

"Ye..s," Jack answered tentatively, both surprised and not a little suspicious at this approach.

"Inspector Bannerman, West Riding Police," he reached into the inside pocket of his jacket and produced a warrant card which he handed to Jack.

Jack studied it carefully, looked at the rather unflattering photograph on the card and then at the man's face. The man smiled ruefully, "Sorry, but that's how we look to police photographers."

Jack was still not convinced; to him strangers on the road were highly suspect; his usual open-hearted, generous view of human nature had been rather eroded in the past twenty-four hours.

The Inspector, recognising the doubt in the younger man's mind, said, "Constable Bainbridge in the village told me I'd probably find you down here, I'd like a chat with you if I may. We can go and see the constable now if you like? Get in, I'll give you a lift up there."

Jack's fears were allayed at the mention of the constable's name and he smiled and got into the car with the Inspector, "I've come across some unusual folk in the last twenty-four hours," he explained.

"That's exactly what I want to talk to you about," the Inspector said as he started the car and drove up the lane. However, instead of going straight into the village main street he pulled into a cart track on the left of the lane and stopped the vehicle.

"Sorry about this cloak and dagger stuff but I need to discuss a few things with you without being observed. I'll be quite straight with you, Mr Warrendale, and tell you why I'm here."

"Well, I guess it's my uncle's disappearance, isn't it?"

"Right, that's what's brought matters to a head, but there are other things which are bothering us. For instance, we've had reports of an increase in the number of strangers seen in the area. Yes, I know it's a tourist area," he went on quickly before Jack could interrupt. "Even allowing for that, there have been unusual sightings reported. All the local constables were instructed to report anything out of the ordinary, and quite frankly, the results have been nothing short of amazing. Then, when your uncle was reported missing, I was sent up here to help with the enquiries. I'll confide in you, Mr. Warrendale, but please keep this to yourself. I'm expecting a man up from London anytime, a Secret Service agent."

Jack expressed his surprise, "Wow," he said, "That serious, is it?"

"Well, they certainly seem to think so. Look," he went on, "I've had Bainbridge's written report and I've just had a word with him. I'd like to know now what you've managed to find out, if anything."

After his initial doubts Jack had rapidly warmed to the Inspector. He seemed to know what he was doing and Jack felt he could confide in him. And sure as hell, Jack thought, he needed someone to confide in. He'd realised at the railway station he could be getting in out of his depth. He had begun to feel distinctly isolated, and he was glad of the opportunity to discuss things openly with someone. Jack told the Inspector everything that had happened from the time he met Ruth on train in London right up the events of this lunchtime when Ruth had arrived in Langham. He also mentioned the unusual behaviour of the vicar, his conversation with Mrs. Thornton, and her story of the nocturnal smugglers.

"Ah, yes, I've already heard about them from the constable; some time ago, in fact."

Good for Bainbridge, Jack thought, most people would have dismissed her fears as an old woman's overactive imagination.

"Tell me," Inspector Bannerman said, "I say, would you mind if I called you, Jack?"

"Not at all," Jack answered immediately.

"Right, I'm Mike, by the way. Oh, and, incidentally, I'm attached to the Special Branch in Leeds."

Jack wasn't sure who, or what, the Special Branch was, but he was nonetheless suitably impressed by the sound of it.

"Now tell me, what do you think was going on at the station this morning, Jack?" Mike asked, stressing the 'you' and looking straight at him.

"God knows," Jack answered quickly. "But I do know that all is not well with Ruth Lancaster. I'd decided the best thing I could do was to open the suitcase before I took it back, and see if there was anything in there which would help explain things."

"I think that's an excellent idea. We'll check it out together and then you can give it back to her this afternoon. I need to keep in the background as much as I can, so if anyone asks we can tell them I'm a friend of yours from London?"

"Right," agreed Jack. "By the way, are you staying in the village?"

"I've been staying at The Flying Dutchman for the last couple of nights, it's not bad there at all. Easy to keep yourself to yourself."

"Why don't you stay up at my uncle's farm, there's plenty of room up there and I'm sure Aunt Dorcas wouldn't mind. It'd look more convincing as well?", Jack suggested.

"I'd love too, if you think it would be all right?" Mike responded enthusiastically.

"I'm sure it will be," said Jack.

Mike produced a one-inch ordnance survey map from the glove compartment and opened it on his knee, "Can you just fill me in on the area, Jack? Before we make a move."

Jack leaned over and pointed out the significant features on the map. He showed Mike the different ways to get to his uncle's farm, and also indicated the route Bergman had followed the previous evening. Mike browsed over the map a few moments longer and then folded it up and put it away. "I'll see you in about half an hour then, up at the farm."

Jack smiled his agreement. "Right, I'll see you then."

He climbed out of the car and walked up the lane to the village. He saw nothing at all untoward, in fact it was very quiet in the main street. He didn't even dare to glance at The Old Crown as he went past, although he did wonder if his passing had been noticed.

His aunt was pleased to see him back so early and, in spite of his protests, immediately started preparing him a sandwich and a pot of tea.

Jack told his aunt that he'd come back for the suitcase, and also that quite surprisingly he'd met a friend of his from London.

"Is it all right if he stays here for a while? He's offered to help me in the search for Uncle Joss," he explained, not altogether untruthfully.

"Of course it is, love. That's very good of him."

"He'll be here in a minute. He just had to make a call in the village."

"Right you are, I'll make him a sandwich as well while I'm at it. I'll bet he'll be hungry as well." She busied herself at the table. Jack watched her for a moment as her grey head bent over the bread board. He was glad he'd asked Mike to stay, it would be much better for his aunt if she was kept busy, even if it was only making sandwiches.

A warning bark from Gemmy sent Jack hurrying to the door and he returned in a few seconds followed by the inspector, now kitted out in hiking gear and carrying a large rucksack.

"That's more like it, Mike", Jack said approvingly, "You look less like a policeman now."

Mike laughed," I must say I feel a lot more comfortable in this outfit."

"Auntie", Jack raised his voice slightly so his aunt could hear him properly. "This is my friend, Mike Bannerman, from London, the chap I mentioned."

They exchanged greetings and shook hands.

"Come and sit down the both of you," his aunt ordered. "I've made a sandwich and a pot of tea, I'll bet you're ready for this." She fussed about with the sugar dish, the milk, the mustard and anything else she could think of, and not until she was satisfied that they had everything they needed, did she leave them at the table and take her own tea and sit in the rocker by the hearth. Jack smiled tolerantly and got stuck into his sandwiches, he hadn't realised how hungry he was. Of course, he thought, he'd missed lunch completely, what with one thing and another.

He'd had chance to study the inspector more closely as they were sitting at the table. He was in his late thirties, Jack guessed, medium height, quite an athletic build, dark hair brushed back, very steady brown eyes, and a ready smile. He reminded Jack of a young bank executive, or one who would eventually be invited onto the board. Anyway, he struck Jack as a chap you could put your trust in.

"What do you think is going on here, Mike?" he asked, between mouthfuls of cheese sandwich.

"Er, well, having heard what you've had to say about Ruth and this mysterious Bergman chap, I'm more convinced now that something underhand is going on. My chief, for instance, was worried about the infiltration of saboteurs from Ireland. He reckoned they could get into the country fairly easily up here, lie low for a while, and perhaps use it as a training area."

"What do you think of that idea?" prompted Jack.

"Not much," Mike remarked quickly. "Why bring them over here untrained? They've plenty of isolation in their own country."

After the snack Jack showed Mike around the house and the spare bedroom which his Aunt had suggested he use. Once upstairs Jack produced Ruth's suitcase from under the bed and Mike removed the leather strap which encircled it.

"I'll bet it's locked," said Mike.

"It is," confirmed Jack. "I tried it the other day. Not to open it," he added hastily. "Just really out of curiosity."

"We'll have to force it, gently though. I don't want it to appear as if it's been opened. Have you got a fairly strong kitchen knife, Jack? It shouldn't be too difficult."

Jack soon returned with a large knife and within a few seconds Mike had gently prised open the catch.

"Now, let's see what we've got here. I'll put everything on the bed as we take it out so we can put it back in the same order."

He carefully removed two woollen sweaters off the top, then a tweed skirt, a folded jacket, some underwear, an evening dress, a couple of blouses and a toilet bag. Jack felt some embarrassment at the thought of handling Ruth's clothes like this but, even so, he was completely absorbed in the task. There was only a blue manila folder left in the bottom of the case now, and disappointment was already building up in Jack's mind. Mike lifted it out with both hands and placed it on the bed. Both men gasped involuntarily at what they now saw in the case. Mike was the first to speak, and then only in a whisper, "What the hell is she doing with that?"

Jack didn't answer, he just stared, a look of disbelief on his face; nestling in the corner of the suitcase was a shiny black metallic revolver.

"A Walther PPK", Mike said, picking up the weapon and removing the magazine. "One of the newer ones. Brand new, if you ask me. Should be a spare magazine somewhere?" he added, feeling about in the bottom of the case. "Ah, here it is", he exclaimed, pulling it out of an elasticated pocket at the side of the case.

"Bloody hell," muttered Jack, recovering his composure. "What do you make of this then, Mike?"

"Well, my guess is, she's either working for the British, or possibly the German government. Let's have a look in this folder."

This was the first time that doubt about Ruth had entered Jack's head. He'd just regarded her, like himself, as an innocent victim of adverse circumstances, and now, look at this, she was as much involved in the shady deals as Bergman and his henchmen.

Meanwhile Mike had spread the documents from the folder on the bed and he called Jack over. "Look at this, Jack. This *is* interesting", he said.

Jack saw at a glance that some of the papers were stamped OHMS on the top and others were marked 'Classified, a few appeared to be just scribbled notes. Mike handed over the letter he had been perusing, "Have a look over that one, Jack. I think that'll give you a good idea of what's going on. It's a memorandum from a colonel in the security branch at the Home Office to one of their field officers."

Jack took the sheaf of papers and sat in a chair by the bedroom window to read it through. On top was a single typed sheet.

From   : *Colonel Stafford, Home Office*

To   :   *Miss Ruth Lancaster, Field Officer*

Proceed to the town of Settle to liaise with local police force regarding sightings of strangers, possibly foreign agents, in the surrounding area. You are to arrest and question anyone suspected of taking photographs, making notes or diagrams of coastal defences, military installations or anything which could be useful to a foreign power. Attached is a recent photograph of a known suspect. Report all movements, if sighted.

You are warned that foreign agents may be armed and dangerous. Good luck.

Jack finished the page and sighed, "Thank God for that anyway, she's one of us". He turned the top sheet over to reveal a six by nine glossy photograph. "Well, well! Would you look at this?". Jack held up the photograph of a man.

"Our benevolent friend, Pastor Bergman", said Mike, "Would you believe it?"

"Well, he had a certain look about him, that man", replied Jack.

"It starting to look as though your Miss Lancaster is the 'man' I said was coming up from London," Mike said, thoughtfully, his attention back on the papers spread out on the bed.

"Something went wrong on the train, and I got involved", said Jack.

"That's about it," agreed Mike. "But they're desperate for the suitcase so I suggest you get it to them as soon as possible. I'm keeping this file out, of course, and the gun. The rest can go back as it was. With any luck they'll think she's just an ordinary tourist."

It took only a few minutes to re-pack the suitcase. The lock snapped closed again and Jack was relieved to see that it did not appear to have been tampered with.

"You get off straight away, Jack," Mike suggested. "Keep your eyes open when you hand it over but do it as naturally as possible. No awkward questions or anything like that." He looked down at the documents again, "We've got a lot of work on here, Jack. London seems to think the Germans are involved, but there's a lot here I can't make head nor tail of."

"Right, I'll get back as soon as I can then." Jack lugged the suitcase down the steps, told his aunt he wouldn't be very long and set off for village once more. Thank God it's the last time I'll be carrying this thing around. But his heart leapt at the thought of seeing Ruth again - but a Secret Service agent? He felt even more of a country bumpkin now than he had done on the train.

Jack walked through the main entrance into the hotel section of The Old Crown. Uncle Joss always referred to this part as the 'posh end o't pub', and its red-carpeted hallway and imposing reception desk certainly gave it an air of distinction. Jack walked along the carpet towards the desk, feeling completely out-of-place, and more than a little self-conscious, in his corduroy trousers and well-worn jumper. He was grateful for the fact that none of the hotel guests were in the foyer at that time.

"Excuse me," he said quietly to the girl behind the desk, who was apparently deep in the study of some important ledger. Jack waited, he knew she knew he was there, and he knew that this was a little charade they were playing. It was called 'putting people in their place'.

"Excuse me," Jack repeated, considerably louder this time, and acutely aware of the coarseness of his own speech.

The girl deigned to look up, her eyes reluctantly leaving the absorbing document. "Can I help you, sir?"

Where in God's name, Jack thought, did they teach people to speak in such a patronising way? "I'd like to see Miss Lancaster, please. I think she's in room twenty-five."

The receptionist consulted the register and then checked the key board behind her. "That's correct, sir. Room twenty-five. Miss Lancaster appears to be in at the moment. Shall I get someone to carry your suitcase?"

"No, no thanks, I can manage."

"First floor, at the end of the corridor, on the left, sir."

Jack mumbled his thanks and made his way across to the staircase on the right, aware that the girl was studying him closely, and he guessed, disapprovingly. He wondered if he'd walked in some cowflap on the way down from the farm and if he'd left a distinctive trail of footprints across the foyer. He grinned to himself at the thought as he mounted the staircase and turned onto the corridor at the top. The luxurious depth of the carpet muffled his footsteps and he moved noiselessly along the corridor scanning the door numbers on his left. His plan to do a little eavesdropping at the door of twenty-five was thwarted, however, by the sudden appearance out of an alcove opposite, of the large figure of Ruth's so-called brother's friend.

"Hello, again," Jack said, with far more warmth than he felt. "Is Ruth in? I've brought her suitcase back." He held it up to show him, in what he realised was a somewhat unnecessary action. Perhaps I am the village idiot, he thought to himself.

"I think so," the man replied, and Jack now noticed the slight foreign sound in the man's voice. "I'll tell her you're here, excuse me." The man knocked twice on the door of twenty-five which opened, more or less immediately, as though the person at the other side had been expecting it.

78

"The gentleman with Ruth's suitcase has arrived," he said through the gap in the doorway.

The door opened wide and Ruth's 'brother' came out, "Ah, that's very kind of you. Come in, please". He ushered Jack into the sitting room. No sign of Ruth, Jack's eyes rapidly scanned the room, revealing nothing unusual that he could see.

"I'm afraid my sister is taking a bath at the moment, but I'll tell her you called, she'll probably want to see you later and express her thanks. Would you like a drink?"

It sounded like a very well-rehearsed speech to Jack and one that owed a lot to some English phrase book for foreigners. Jack thought about the offer for a second but he felt uncomfortable with the other man standing behind him and he knew he wouldn't find much out here; they were obviously well-prepared for his visit. Jack's main worry was that he might reveal something of his recently acquired knowledge.

No, thanks very much," he said, smiling at the man. "I've another call to make. I'll see Ruth later." He turned to go, and the 'friend' opened the door for him. "Goodbye," he called over his shoulder, "Nice to meet you," he added, as he strolled nonchalantly away along the corridor. Once around the corner he slowly exhaled a pent-up volume of air which seemed to have built up in his lungs, and, as he descended the staircase to the hotel foyer, he surreptitiously wiped his sweating palms on his trouser sides.

The first question Mike asked when Jack got back to the farm was, "How many were there?"

"At least three I should guess," Jack estimated. "I saw the two youngish men, and Ruth wasn't in sight, so presumably she was being guarded by a third. I didn't see the vicar at all so it could have been him, I suppose?" Jack went through the events at the hotel in as much detail as he could and Mike was obviously pleased with the outcome.

"Good, well done, Jack, From what you say they don't seem to suspect we're on to them. We've just got to make sure we keep it that way, until we do know what they're up to. Were they armed, by the way?"

Jack cursed under his breath; he'd never thought about that. To Mike he said, "I'm sorry, I don't really know. They were both wearing jackets, but I just didn't notice if there were any significant bulges or anything, but they could have been armed." He paused for a second, "Wait a minute, though, the man I met on the corridor at first had one hand in his jacket pocket, like this," and Jack demonstrated with his hand," but he looked quite natural with it."

"All right, we must assume they are. How else would they have got Ruth to co-operate? Unless, of course," he remarked thoughtfully, "they're holding someone hostage. You know, parents, or sister perhaps? I'll get the Leeds police to check it out when we've decided what we're going to do at this end. First there's another photo I want you to look at." He passed over a photograph. "You'll recognise our clerical friend", he smiled. "But have you seen the other chap about? He's Irish, his name's Brendan O'Brady, a fully fledged member of the IRA and very dangerous by all accounts. His nickname's 'Bob'."

Jack shook his head, it was a good likeness of Bergman, if there could be anything good about that slimy worm, thought Jack. The other man was a complete stranger.

"Have a look at this then, Jack, and see if you can make anything of it." He handed Jack a sheet of paper; a loose-leaf page from the folder by the look of it, and Jack assumed the notes were in Ruth's handwriting.

Jack scanned the page. Mike was right, it wasn't easy to follow They read more like unrelated jottings than structured notes, as if Ruth had been scribbling down reminders as she listened to someone speaking. He read the notes aloud to try and help himself concentrate and focus his mind on the page.

Inter.w'less mess 14/5

Brigante One   East: 140deg.uber drei mensch, gerade aus

1: drei grun   1000 10 km.

2: zwei grun   800

3 ein grun   730

alles..ordnung...fertig.. wiedersehen, uber und aus!.

Mike leaned over his shoulder, "Does it mean anything to you?"

"Well, struggling with my schoolboy German, it would seem to be an intercepted wireless message that's been picked up, say on the 14th May," Jack postulated. "East and then 140 degrees. gerade aus means straight on, doesn't it?"

"Right," Mike agreed. "That's what I gathered. What about this Brigante One thing though?"

"Some kind of call sign, do you think? The Brigantes were an ancient British tribe who used to live on the top of Ingleborough, if that's any good."

"Really? "exclaimed Mike. "They must have been a tough old bunch."

"I don't think they lived up there all the time, probably just went up for their holidays, or when the Romans were after them," Jack said with a laugh.

"You see those figures there, starting at 1000 ," pointing at the notes, "What are they, distances? Contours?"

"Well they're not contours, not with a thirty on it. Wait a minute, if they were heights the Germans would have them in metres wouldn't they?", Jack concluded," so what's 730 metres in feet."

Mike shook his head, "God, knows. About three times as much?" he speculated hopefully.

"I'll tell you in a minute," said Jack, filling the scrap of paper in front of him with figures. Mike waited expectantly for the outcome. Jack looked up, "2373", he said jubilantly.

"So?" said Mike, "What's so special about that?"

"Only that 2373 feet is the height of Ingleborough!"

"Is it, by God? Now that is interesting," he leaned over the notes again. "We're getting somewhere now, this is some kind of route which finishes on the top of Ingleborough, isn't it?" Mike's voice had a ring of excitement to it now. "These are descending altitudes from 1000 metres, aren't they? And what about this 'drei mensch', it means three people, or three men, is that the number in the group, do you think?"

"I know where the three men are," Jack remarked confidently.

"You do?" queried Mike in some disbelief.

"Yes, they're quite well-known around here, they've been standing there for ages". Seeing a scornful look flash across Mike's face he hurriedly went on, "The Three Men of Gragareth. They're three cairns on the hillside above Beck Fell, a bit to the north west of where we are now."

Mike looked at Jack with undisguised admiration on face, "Well done, Jack. I think you've cracked it. If that bearing of 140 degrees ties up we've got the exact route."

"A route for what, exactly? Oh, I see," said Jack consulting the notes again, "A flight path, you think, and these are the heights coming down to Ingleborough."

"Could they land an aeroplane on top, do you think?"

"Well someone's done it before, I've heard. The top's about half a mile in circumference but it's a bit rough in parts. I can't say I'd fancy it though. Yes, they could if they picked their spot and cleared the ground, and if the weather and the wind were right."

Mike fished in his rucksack pocket and produced his map and a magnetic compass. "Show me where the Three Men are, Jack, and let's test the theory." He spread out the map on the floor and both men crouched over it.

"This is the valley up Beck Fell," Jack followed it up with his finger, "and this is Gragareth on the right. The Three Men are just about there, just above that farm building." His forefinger rested on Beck Fell House.

Mike placed the straight edge of the compass on the spot and rotated the housing to 140 degrees, a look of disappointment flashed across his face, "No, it can't be that, it's well down the valley," he said quietly. "Oh, wait a minute, I'm stupid. This'll be a true bearing, won't it? Let's see, working from large land to small map, subtract the declension, which is about 12 degrees."

He fiddled with the compass housing again and placed it on the map. "Eureka!" he shouted, looking up at Jack with a broad grin on his face. "Bang on. Look, it points directly to Ingleborough." He sat back on his haunches with a smile of satisfaction on his face. He turned and picked up the notes from the bed, "Right, now which are the high points between here," he said, with one finger on the Three Men and another on Ingleborough, " and here?"

"Well, there's Gragareth itself ," Jack traced the route across with his finger, stopping to draw attention to the significant features. "There's the valley of Kingsdale, then a ridge between Ewes Cross and Scale Fell which goes up to Whernside here, then across this valley, Chapel-le-dale, and over these limestone pavements to the summit of Ingleborough, here".

"Great, Jack. It all ties in. Look at this!", Mike exclaimed, holding up Ruth's notes. " Three green, that'll be lights, of course, on this first ridge, then two green lights on this one and finally one light to indicate the summit, and presumably they'll have a landing strip marked out up there as well. The plane comes up the valley of the Lune at three thousand feet," Mike used his right hand to represent the aeroplane's flight. "It turns through 140 degrees when the pilot sees the lights on the Three Men, then reduces height gradually and just follows the direction lights over the ridges to Ingleborough. Very neat, very thorough."

"What do we do now, then?" queried Jack.

"Well, I reckon we've got to act pretty quickly because I've a feeling this operation has already started. Really we need more men, but I don't think we've the time to get them." Mike was thinking aloud, Jack realised, rather than actually talking to him. "We have a theory at the moment, that's all, no actual proof. It might even be a hoax, a distraction. We need to establish some facts before I can ask for reinforcements, that's obvious." He wandered around the room for a minute or two, deep in thought, and Jack didn't interrupt him.

"Right, Jack, this is my suggestion. Let me have your ideas as I go along, you know the area much better than I do. As I see it we need to do two things. First, check this theory about the flight path and the landing zone; I'll look a right bloody fool if it's just an elaborate hoax. Secondly, we have to keep an eye on what's happening down at the Crown. We need to know if the party moves at all, and also that Ruth Lancaster is not in any immediate danger."

Jack's self esteem had risen tremendously since his contact with Mike. The way the latter had taken him into his confidence, and the friendly manner in which he treated Jack as an equal, with no intrusive hint of rank or position, had given the younger man a degree of self-confidence he'd not felt before.

"Well, it seems fairly obvious, Mike. I'd better go up the hill and check things there, and you go down to the village and watch the villains. You can get the constable to help you, as well," and, as an afterthought, he added, "You've also got to check with the police in Leeds, haven't you? About Ruth's family, I mean."

"Yes, right, I'm glad you reminded me. What bothers me a bit, Jack, is the way I'm involving you in all this. It might be dangerous, they're no mugs, this lot."

"Look," Jack said quickly, "I am involved, aren't I? It's my uncle that's gone missing, and I'll bet that's connected with all this, and then there's Ruth and the suitcase on the train, and you need someone who knows the countryside round here. I reckon I can find out what we need to know without being seen."

Mike smiled, "You've made your case, Jack, and I'm glad you're with me; I just had to mention it." He glanced at his watch, "We've another hour or so of light left, so I'll get down to the village, and you go up the mountain, and for God's sake keep your head down, and take care".

Jack grinned, "And you."

"I may be here when you get back, but if not check with Bainbridge in the village. I'll bring him up-to-date when I get down there."

Whilst they had been talking Jack had fished out his hiking boots from under the bed and put them on. He took his thick jacket and his cap from the wardrobe. "Right, that's me ready. I'll borrow Uncle Joss's field glasses as well. They'll be useful."

He clumped down the staircase behind Mike, "We're just going out again, Auntie", he said as his aunt looked up from her chair. " We don't know how long we'll be so don't wait up for us. We've got a lot of information to follow up."

"Right-o, love. I'll leave some sandwiches out for your supper, you'll be peckish when you get back. I'll put 'em under a plate on the table, so don't forget."

Jack looked at Mike and, unseen by his aunt, raised his eyebrows in mock despair. Mike grinned back, and turning to the old lady said in his most charming manner, "That's very thoughtful of you Mrs. Warrendale, thank you very much."

When they got outside Jack turned to Mike and said in a low voice, "If this job goes on for any length of time, you know, we'll be like a couple of Billy Bunters. She's a lovely woman but she thinks it's her duty to fill us up with food all the time."

"Well, there's a lot worse things than that," said Mike laughing.

They wished each other good luck and separated; Mike taking the track round the back of the farm to the village, and Jack heading downhill and across the valley to a lane on the other slope, well away from the direct route up the mountain.

Eight

Ingleborough summit, Yorkshire Dales, 6th July 1939

Jack walked casually up the pasture on the valley side. If he was being observed he wanted it to appear as though he was simply checking the sheep. In his flat cap and rough jacket, and carrying his uncle's crook, he felt very much a part of the rural scene. Each time he stopped, ostensibly to check on sheep or the condition of the walls, his eyes had surreptitiously swept the valley sides, but he'd seen no one at all. Once over the wall at the top and onto the walled green track, and out-of-sight of anyone below, he was able to move more quickly and soon reached the gate that led on to the open moor.

Avoiding the limestone outcrops he cut directly across the grassy hillocks in the direction of Ingleborough, aiming to cross the main track about half way up. On the top of one grassy knoll he paused, lay down on the springy turf, took out his uncle's binoculars and swept the slopes above and below. Not a sign of anyone on the massive rounded hill in front of him, now darkening rapidly in the shadow of the setting sun. His slow sweep of the lower slopes stopped abruptly at one point, and he adjusted the focus to sharpen the image. A small group of people; perhaps four or five, Jack couldn't quite make out the exact number. He wiped his eyes and tried again. No, still impossible to tell, they were too close together. The group was standing on the rim of a depression in the moor between Gaping Gill and the track out of Devil's Gill. Jack knew precisely where they were, there was a crater of collapsed limestone there, in one corner of which was the narrow entrance to Bar Pot, itself a back entrance to the huge Gaping Gill system. The sink hole was almost wedge-shaped, dropping from moor level to a depth of thirty to forty feet; the entrance to the pothole being visible in the bottom right hand corner. Sheer sided rock faces ringed the shake hole on three sides, but a sloping track from one corner gave a relatively easy access to the cave mouth.

Jack had been down Bar Pot some years ago. The descent involved a fair bit of difficult ladder-work, he remembered ruefully, especially coming out. He smiled at the recollection and forced his mind back to the present. A caving group? A party of hikers resting on the way down? Nazi spies? He almost laughed out loud at the ridiculous sound of the last one. But he realised, becoming serious very quickly, that it was, in all probability, the correct conclusion.

Jack moved stealthily now, keeping very low and, wherever possible using the lie of the land to conceal himself from the view of the people below. He scurried across the main track on the saddle between the shoulder of Little Ingleborough and the summit. He was making for the crags of millstone grit which ringed the summit perimeter like a rocky necklace. Jack found it particularly warm work even though the sun had now gone down, and he was glad when he had scrambled up through the last of the rocks and was able to throw himself down and recover his breath.

He raised his head carefully to look along the summit plateau; he could see the conspicuous cairn of stones to his left, and the makeshift stone shelter to the right of it, but in the fading light there was no sign of people.

Jack rolled over on to his back and looked out over Morecambe Bay, the sands now shimmering in the reflected light from the evening sky. Wisps of cirrus, olive and mauve, like bedroom curtains gently drawn across the evening sky, were now obscuring the sun's flamboyant colours. As the warmth went out of the sky, Jack felt the first chill of night enclose him, psychological perhaps, but in spite of his sweating ascent, he shivered and buttoned up his jacket. He swept the lower slopes with the field glasses but could see no movement on the main track up.

He crawled along the rim of the plateau to better his position to look at the stone shelter. This, he knew, was little more than a stone wall but it did provide some protection from the wind, and if anybody was going to be up here at night this is where they would be. He was wrong; when he cautiously raised his head over the rocky parapet he could clearly see the figures of two men moving away from him towards the north west edge of the summit. They were working independently, crouching occasionally, obviously either clearing the ground or fixing landing lights. Very busy and very organised, Jack thought, as he watched intently through the glasses. He knew he couldn't get much nearer than this and keep his cover; the cliffs further round to the north west of the summit were quite precipitous and fell sheer for hundreds of feet.

Voices to his right froze him with fear. Oh hell, he cursed, what an idiot. What a fool. He prayed he'd not been seen and not even daring to look around, slowly lowered himself to the grass. There were no obvious cries of alarm, and Jack could hear the sound of footsteps now and the occasional mutter of conversation. People were coming up the path from below, Jack shrank into the rocks, he didn't think he'd been silhouetted against the night sky but it was a near thing, and he was absolutely furious with himself for being so careless. He knew he could have ruined the whole operation, and the thought of the disgrace sent him cold with shame.

Two figures appeared over the rim of the summit to the right, as Jack, lying flat on the grass brooded on his own stupidity. One of the men was considerably shorter than the other and both were carrying suitcases. Neither was Bergman, he noted, he felt he could recognise that figure anywhere now. The walkers headed straight for the shelter and Jack saw their arms raise in greeting to the two men working on the summit.

Jack's unbounded relief at not being discovered had the salutary effect of now making him ultra-cautious. He peered over the edge of the crag like a watchful rabbit, glasses trained on the men but ears alert to the sounds of the night. An evening mist was beginning to form in the deeper valleys to his left, he noticed, and he instinctively pulled up his coat collar protectively. Something was going to happen soon, he guessed; the men were together now and there was an air of expectancy in their movements.

What happened then, however, still took Jack by surprise. A brilliant beam of light flashed out across the valley towards the north west away from Jack's hiding place. It lasted only a second and then was repeated twice more in rapid succession; Jack raised himself up to see the effects of the signal, because signal it obviously was, and he was not mistaken. An answering light flashed three times across the valley from the lower slopes of the Whernside ridge, and then farther away yet another three flashes of light marked, what Jack guessed would be the Gragareth ridge. Jack was jubilant, just as we'd worked out, he thought. He had secretly nursed strong doubts about the possibility of landing an aeroplane on the summit of Ingleborough. He knew from experience how severe the weather could be up here; even in summer you frequently got dense cloud on the summit, and there was always the possibility of high winds. Tonight, however, the night was still and clear, and it looked as though this highly organised team were about to do the improbable and guide an aeroplane down.

Jack watched intently, fascinated by the drama unfolding before him. The men had been galvanised into action again; he saw them pointing into the sky to the north-west, and training his field glasses in that direction, he too picked up the tiny speck of light high above the darkening ridges.

The figures on the summit moved quickly from point to point igniting two parallel lines of flares, or paraffin lamps or whatever they were. A single green light, on the north west rim of the plateau, shone out over the valley. Looking across the dale onto the neighbouring ridge, probably nearly a thousand feet below him, Jack could see two green lights in direct line for the summit; the flight path was lit and the plane was coming in. He felt the nervous tension.

Better him than me, thought Jack. He could see the dark shape of the single winged plane, unlit now and descending in a silent glide over the valley. He started slightly at the noise when the pilot restarted the engine about a quarter of a mile away. The plane looked much bigger than Jack had expected and he could see the angle of the wings move as the pilot lined up for his descent. It seemed to be coming in very fast and heading directly for Jack's position. He's going too fast, he's going to overshoot, Jack started to panic. Then he saw the wing flaps come down, the nose of the plane tilt up a split second before the wheels touched down, then an enormous cloud of dust and rubble momentarily obscured the plane from his view. When it had cleared Jack could see that it was now stationary and the men were running towards it. Jack had been completely transfixed during the landing and he now felt as elated as the men on the ground. Why, he never thought to question, because they were no friends of his; probably the daring achievement itself appealed to his sense of adventure. It suddenly all seemed totally unreal; it was just like being at the pictures and he was sitting in the front stalls.

Two people had emerged from the side door of the plane; there were greetings and handshakes, Jack could see as much through the glasses, and two other men climbed on board, presumably, Jack surmised, the ones who had just come up the track.

The plane's engine had been kept running and it now taxied round and faced the illuminated strip of ground. With an ear-blasting roar, as the pilot opened the throttle, the aircraft shot forward along the slightly downward sloping ground towards the edge of the summit. In a cloud of dust and flying stones it left the mountain, dropped below the level of the summit for a moment, causing all the observers, Jack included, to stand on tiptoe to follow its progress. For a few seconds they looked down on the upper fuselage of the plane but then it rapidly gained height, and sped across the night sky in the direction of Kingsdale and Gragareth.

All the men on the summit, including Jack, were completely engrossed in the plane's departure. Their eyes, as though mesmerised, had followed its line of flight until it became just a dot of light as turned east in the night sky and headed out towards the Irish Sea.

Nine

The slopes of Ingleborough, Yorkshire Dales, 6ᵗʰ July 1939

It was a real anticlimax when the plane disappeared from view. It was as though the star of the show had left the stage, and the audience, and stage-hands, were left behind to tidy up in darkness. For a brief moment they'd been at the centre of the action; in the limelight almost, and the empty arena was noticeably a much bleaker place. The lights were out, the show was over, the men were scurrying about with equipment and Jack was frozen to the marrow. He envied the landing party their opportunity to work and keep warm whilst he restricted himself to walking on the spot and high-rising his knees to ease the stiffness.

Jack went over the sequence of events in his mind. He wanted to be able to give Mike a coherent report about the landing; in fact, he couldn't wait to see his face when he told him. Glancing at his watch he realised it was still only 9:20pm; he felt as though he'd been up there a week. The aeroplane, he worked out, had been on the summit only a matter of minutes, five or six at the most. He was still filled with a profound admiration for the skill and courage of the pilot, and the sleek efficiency of the landing party.

On our side, he thought counting on his fingers, there's me, Mike, Bob Bainbridge and, struggling for inspiration, added facetiously, Mrs. Thornton, the all-seeing eye. He smiled to himself at the thought, but couldn't help thinking that the scales seemed overwhelmingly weighted in favour of the streamlined organisation he'd just witnessed.

The men on the summit had removed all traces of the landing gear now and were heading towards the rocks in Jack's direction. He could tell by their stooped postures that they were struggling with heavy loads. He sank down between a crevice in the rocks and watched as they concealed the containers amongst the rocky outcrop some twenty yards to his left. The whole lot was then covered by a dark groundsheet and loose stones piled on top. When the men were satisfied with their efforts at concealment they moved slowly in a wide sweep search across the landing zone towards the shelter. Confident, apparently, that all traces of their presence had been removed the men, each carrying a case or a rucksack, headed for the track on the eastern edge of the summit and disappeared from view in the direction of Gaping Gill and the village.

Jack levered himself to his feet, stretched himself and looked around. The plateau was cold, dark, desolate and deserted. He just had one more job to do and then he could get off this bleak inhospitable spot and get down to the warmth of the farm, and his aunt's sandwiches. The very thought warmed him and he strode quickly over to the hidden cache and lifted the tarpaulin sheet. As he thought, there were boxes containing an assortment of paraffin lamps, an aldis lamp, coloured filters, wires, a large battery, a wireless set and a couple of jerrycans. One glance was quite sufficient for his needs and he replaced the cover and set off after the other men. He knew he could catch them up pretty quickly, especially if he kept to the track.

Sure enough some ten or so minutes later he saw the beam of a flashlight about two hundred yards in front of him. The group was just dropping over the crest of the shoulder which overlooked the steep slope leading towards the chasm of Gaping Gill.

Jack kept the same distance between himself and the group in front. The flashlight was only being used occasionally but Jack found it a useful indication of both route and distance and he was reassured by that. It would be ridiculous at this stage, and knowing what he knew, if he blundered into the back of the group and was captured. Jack cringed at the thought of the ignominy of that occurrence.

A quarter of an hour later Jack was walking on level ground. The men had not taken the route to Gaping Gill, but had taken the track to the right which led to Devil's Gill, and eventually past the farm and down to the village. Smugglers in the moonlight, Jack thought, how right you were, Mrs. Thornton.

Jack yawned, he hadn't realised how tired he was, and hungry too. It had been a long, action-packed day with a fair amount of nervous tension, in one way and another. Was it only this morning that he'd met Ruth at the station? He was reminiscing, quite pleasantly absorbed in his own thoughts when he was brought up short by the sound of voices very close on his right. He froze in mid-stride and crouched down on the track. Where the hell were they? His eyes flashed about desperately. Surely to God he hadn't overrun them? No sign of them anywhere, no flashlights, just voices. It wasn't an ambush, he realised with relief, because the voices continued at the same conversational level.

When Jack's initial panic had subsided and he'd checked his bearings he guessed what had happened. The group he had been following had not gone down the track towards the village at all; they were in the crater leading to Bar Pot. Jack could see the silhouette of the ash trees which clung precariously amongst the limestone clints around the edge. This particular shake-hole, or swallow holes, as they are sometimes called, was quite large and the stream which had originally formed the system had moved back up the valley, and for the time being was the one that dropped 360 feet in vertical fall into the depths of Gaping Gill.

Jack approached the steep edge of the depression with great care. He knew there was a sheer rock face at this side and also that there was sufficient cover amongst the limestone outcrop to conceal his presence. He wriggled slowly and carefully along one of the grykes until he could look over the drop of forty feet into the hollow beneath. He had the grandstand view, if not the comfort.

Below him, in a circle of light were five men, four of them wearing carbide headlamps which illuminated the face of the fifth ... Bergman. All, except the latter, were wearing overalls and helmets and were obviously preparing to go underground. The discussion, which had first attracted Jack's attention, now seemed to be finished, and the men began to move their cases towards the narrow cave opening. They disappeared from Jack's view, one by one, like rats down a drainpipe, he thought, leaving only Bergman on the surface. The beam of his flashlight swept around the hollow and Jack drew back instinctively, even though he was well out of sight.

Jack heard Bergman stumble up the stony path at the far side of the depression and onto the main path to the village. Jack waited a minute before he raised his head to watch the man's light weaving its way down the rocky defile.

Jack leaned back against a rock and waited until Bergman was well out of the way. Although he wouldn't be going the same way as the vicar he didn't want to take any chances with that chap about; he was as clever as a box of monkeys, Jack thought, to use one of his aunt's favourite expressions. No, Jack would take the short cut over the top of the hill and through the fields at the back of his uncle's farm; he could be there in five minutes.

Jack glanced quickly to his right, he'd thought he'd seen a movement amongst the jumble of limestone rocks to his right. There was someone there. His blood seemed to freeze, he kept rigidly still, his heart beating twenty to the dozen, should he run like hell or face him and fight? He decided the former option was the most sensible, if he could just get to the track he reckoned he could outrun most people. He turned and wriggled away quietly on his stomach and was just getting his feet in position for a flying start when he heard his name being whispered.

"Jack...Jack, for God's sake..it's me"

Jack turned his head, he could now make out the shape of a person.

"It's me...Mike", the hoarse voice repeated.

Relief flooded through Jack's body, "Oh, Mike, you frightened me to death," he whispered. "Am I glad to see you?"

"Me too you. I've been watching you for the past ten minutes, just praying you wouldn't give your position away. Come on," he said taking

96

Jack's arm and leading him away from the edge, "Let's get the hell out of here. Which is the best way to the farm?"

Jack led the way over the back and Mike followed. When they were well clear of the pothole Mike came alongside Jack. "Quite an eventful evening, wouldn't you say?" he said, a smile on his face.

"That's the understatement of the year", Jack replied slowly, looking at his companion. "I've been amazed, surprised, terrified, shocked, frozen and scared witless, and that's just by you."

Mike laughed out loud, "Yes, sorry about that. Let's get down to the farm and you can tell me all about it."

Ten

Langham, Yorkshire Dales, 6th July 1939

"Right, Jack," said Mike when they were seated in front of the fire in the farm kitchen, steaming pots of tea in their hands and a pile of sandwiches between them. "Let's hear what you managed to find out?"

It took Jack some time and, apart from the occasional exclamation of surprise, Mike kept very quiet, his eyes rivetted on the younger man's face. When Jack had finished, Mike put his head in his hands, then wiped his forehead with both hands and looked at Jack. "Bloody hell, what are we up against here?" he queried, "The whole German army *and* the Luftwaffe?"

Mike briefly told Jack what he had been doing that evening. How he had confided in the constable and enlisted his help; the telephone calls he had made, to Skipton to call up police reinforcements; to Leeds Police to check out the safety of Ruth's parents, and to the Home Office in London to inform them of Ruth's capture. He told Jack how Bob Bainbridge had kept watch on Bergman and his men from the tap room of the Crown, and how, when they left, he, Mike, had followed as the three of them had taken Ruth up Devil's Gill and, eventually, into the cave near where he'd met Jack later that evening.

"Good God," Jack couldn't help himself interrupting at that stage, "She's not down there as well, is she?"

"I'm afraid so, old lad," Mike confirmed sympathetically. "It's my guess that your uncle might be down there also."

"Mmm, that is a bit of a worry. It's not easy to get down. There's two pitches in there and one of them's a long one."

"You've been in there?" queried Mike in surprise.

"Aye, a couple of times, you can get through into the main chamber of Gaping Gill from there."

"Good, that's worth knowing. I'm going to need all the information I can get." Mike took a notebook out of his pocket and jotted down some figures. "You say you saw lights on the next ridge, didn't you? I wonder where they keep the equipment for that signal?"

Jack nodded his head in affirmation. "There are plenty of places around there, sheep folds, old barns, limestone pavements."

"And you saw lights on Gragareth?" Mike added.

"Yes, just one though, I reckon the main lights will be near the Three Men".

"I'm just trying to work out the numbers we're up against," Mike said in explanation. "Two went up with Bergman, four came off the top with you, and there must be at least two at each of the two other signalling points. That makes ten, plus Bergman, that's eleven we're dealing with. There might be more for all we know. Oh, by the way, Jack, I forgot to mention this earlier, but Bob Bainbridge found out that Bergman had made a trip out to Beck Fell this afternoon. He took a taxi, apparently, and spent a couple of hours out there, so that ties in with our calculations."

Changing the subject slightly Mike went on, "I'm getting to like Bob Bainbridge, you know. He looks like a simple country bobby, especially on his bike, but he's much sharper than he looks and he's a real asset. We could do with more like him; as it is there are ten men, plus a sergeant, coming up to the railway station for ten o'clock in the morning. They'll be in plain clothes and I've asked Bob to meet them and keep them out of sight down there in the stationmaster's office."

"Will they be armed?" Jack asked.

"Well, that's what I asked for," smiled Mike. "But knowing the police they'll probably come up with muzzle-loading muskets and half-a-dozen pikestaffs. I could do with getting in touch with the nearest Territorial Army

100

barracks to see if they've any men they can spare. He looked at his watch, "Well, it's after eleven, it's too late to do anything now, anyway. We'll make an early start in the morning, there's a lot to do."

Jack nodded his agreement, "I wonder if they'll try and take Ruth out in that aeroplane?"

"Yes, that's a point, I suppose they might," Mike didn't want to dwell on the other possibilities so he carried on outlining his plans for the following day. "We need to check the signalling points on Gragareth, I'm looking forward to meeting the Three Men," he smiled. "Then there's the middle one on er, Scale Fell, is that it, Jack?" he glanced up at Jack for confirmation.

"Scales Moor," Jack corrected. "Well, somewhere between there and Ewes Cross, with the compass bearing we can get the exact line across the ridge, and presumably it'll be at the highest point on that line."

"Right, that's all right then," Mike said mentally ticking off the various points. "Then there's just the extra men to sort out..", his voice tailed off as his mind considered other possible lines of action. After a second or two he looked up, "You look tired out, Jack. Time to turn in, I reckon, we'll sort it out tomorrow."

Mike didn't go to bed immediately, however, he had no wish to. He gazed out of the window for a long time, deep in thought. The moonlit landscape, silent, still and unreal under its silver sheen was the ideal background for his purposes. He wanted time to analyse the situation and consider all the possibilities. He felt the weight of responsibility lying very heavily on his shoulders at that moment. The operation was far bigger than he'd ever imagined; he was in charge and his decisions were vital. He had to get his plans perfectly clear in his own mind, before he started issuing orders to others. It was also important, he felt, to work out a series of contingency plans in case things didn't run quite as smoothly as intended.

Jack, in contrast, slept the sleep of the exhausted that night. He snuggled down, elated at the progress they'd made, and pleased with the part he'd played in it. In the comfort of his bed he was going to enjoy reliving the experience. Fatigue, however, decided otherwise, and after a very short struggle, he went out like a light switched off on a bare mountain.

Eleven

Langham, Yorkshire Dales, 7th July 1939

Jack was awakened next morning by the sound of his aunt preparing breakfast. He saw from his watch on the bedside table that it was 6:30 am. God, he thought, I've only just come to bed.

He knew his aunt and uncle always started the day early, but he hung on to the warmth of his bed for another quarter of an hour until he heard Mike, in the adjacent room, getting up.

They breakfasted well on bacon and eggs and fried bread, and finished off with toast and Marmite. Aunt Dorcas fussed about the whole while and made sure they had enough of everything. Over coffee, whilst Dorcas was washing-up at the sink in the corner, Mike lowered his voice and said confidentially to Jack, "I'm banking on the same procedure being repeated tonight, you know. You see, everything's still set up on the mountain, the lights, the wireless, all the gear. This spell of good weather is expected to last for a few days. I think they do about three or four flights, change over their agents or something, and then lie low, perhaps for months."

"Seems likely, that," agreed Jack. "I suppose they like a full moon so they can find their way about easier."

"Mmm," murmured Mike thoughtfully, "If the plane doesn't land tonight we'll nab as many as we can anyway, but I would like to get the lot, including the plane and the pilot."

It was a fine morning giving the promise of another warm sunny day and the two men enjoyed the walk down to the village. Constable Bainbridge was in his shirtsleeves at the kitchen window as they went through the gate. He opened the door, his red cheerful face full of smiles.

"'Morning, gentlemen. Come in." He ushered them into the tiny parlour, "Sit yourselves down, I'll just get some tea organised." They heard him talking to his wife in the kitchen and then he returned and squeezed himself into a tub chair by the window, "Nothing doing over yonder so far this morning," he said, nodding his head in the direction of The Old Crown. "But yon vicar were in late last night, he didn't get back until nigh on eleven o'clock, on 'is own he were, an' all."

"Right, well done, Bob," Mike said, "We've got a bit of news for you too." He exchanged glances with Jack and smiled. They were disturbed briefly by Mrs Bainbridge bringing in a loaded tea-tray, "Morning gentlemen, grand day, isn't it?" They agreed with her." See to 'em, Robert," she said to her husband, "frame yourself" and with that instruction she bustled out. The constable smiled good-naturedly and poured out the tea for them.

When they were settled again Mike started talking; quietly and methodically he outlined all that had happened the previous evening. During the next five minutes the constable's face expressed the full range of emotions of which the human countenance is capable. Jack sat there and watched, feeling like some theatrical impresario conducting an audition for some aspiring mime actor.

"Well I never", he managed to say when Mike had finished. He shook his head in wonderment, "Well, I'm fair 'capped, I am that."

Fearing these expressions of amazement could go on for some time, Mike butted in, "This morning me and Jack are going to check out the other two signalling points. So I want you, Bob, to drive us out to Beck Fell, and leave us there until we ring you up for a lift to the next one. While we're out there I want you to take charge at the railway station. When the chaps get there keep 'em out of sight and wait to hear from us. Is that clear?"

"Right sir, perfectly clear. I'll go and get your car from the garage and bring it round to the back."

It took only about thirty minutes for the Rover to reach Beckley, a small hamlet just over the county border in Lancashire. There were not more than a dozen houses in the tiny settlement, which owed its development to the stream which had carved its way down from the higher reaches of Beck Fell. PC Jim Birkwith was the sole agent of law and order in this place, and his beat extended over an area which took in all the outlying farms within a five mile radius. He was a well-built man, favoured a brutally short haircut, almost en brosse. Jack guessed he would be in his early forties. He welcomed Bob with a big smile and rushed out to greet him when he saw the car pull up at his gate.

"Hello Bob. Where've you been for the last couple of months? I haven't seen you since that do in Settle, end of May wasn't it?"

Bainbridge smiled and shook hands with his colleague, but ignored the questions and introduced Jack and Mike. At the mention of Mike's rank the constable immediately became serious and led them into a pokey room which seemed to serve as both office and dining room. He hurriedly removed a tray containing breakfast remains and motioned them to sit down in the straight-backed wooden chairs which lined the wall as though waiting for a class of schoolchildren to arrive.

When the door was closed Mike asked the Constable if anything unusual had been reported recently.

He frowned thoughtfully for a second or two, and then said hesitantly, "Well...er there was one thing, only yesterday it were. It were old Mr Shaw, he farms up the valley, on the Casterton side. I thought he were kidding me, he asked me if I'd been to the party the other night. I asked him which party? And he said the one at Beck Fell Farm." The constable paused and looked at Mike, "I don't know whether this is important, sir ?"

"Oh, it is, believe me, constable." interrupted Mike. "Please go on."

"Well, he said he'd seen coloured lights and things on the hillside at the back o' Sam and Hannah Craven's the night before last. To be honest, he's knocking on a bit, and I thought he must 'a' been dreaming, or possibly drinking a bit too much these days."

"Did he say what time he saw the lights? Or what colour they were?" Mike enquired.

"He didn't mention the colour at all, but he said it were just as it were getting dark, about 9 o'clock, or just after. I were going to have a ride up there today to see if they was all right."

"Do you usually do that?" Mike asked quickly.

"Aye, about once a week," the constable explained . "I have a round, you know. I try and keep in touch with all these hill farms at least once a week."

"Excellent, I want you to make a visit as soon as possible this morning, constable."

"Is there something I should know about, sir?" Birkwith asked quickly with a worried look on his face.

"We're not sure, but there might be. There's something unusual going on that area which might involve the house, but then again it might not. That's what I'm hoping you'll find out. But, and I do stress this constable, you must act exactly the same as you always do, no awkward questions, no poking around. There might be other people up there and if so they mustn't suspect anything. Just go in and come out and report back here. Do not take any action yourself. Is that understood? It's very important."

"Understood, sir," he leapt to his feet, and Jack thought for a minute that he was going to run up the hillside there and then. "I'll just get my bike out of the shed and get going."

"Good, as soon as you can, constable, and remember, keep it natural and don't do anything out of the ordinary."

Birkwith hurried out and Mike turned to Bob Bainbridge, "I'd like you to drive back into the village now, if you don't mind, Bob. Make the reinforcements comfortable, but don't let them wander around, for God's sake. I'll ring you when we've finished here. Is that all right?"

"Right, sir." He got to his feet, nodded to Jack, "See you later then."

Mike spread his map on the table and the two men bent over it. "If we walk up the beck here," Jack indicated with his forefinger, "and cross here and make our way up this side of the valley to this road here, we can look right across to the farmhouse and the Three Men, on the hillside, there."

"Is there enough cover up there, do you think? If they're in the house they'll be watching the approaches like hawks."

"We'll be all right in the valley because it's out of sight of the farmhouse," Jack explained. " And there are trees and bushes on the edge of the road, so really it's just this short bit up the hillside here where we'll have to be careful. We'll just split up and look as much like farmers as we can."

It was as Jack had said, they felt sure they'd reached the high ground on the other side of the valley without raising any suspicions. Seated at the side of the narrow lane, concealed by weeds and low bushes Jack and Mike were peering through field glasses at the squat grey farm building on the opposite slope. Smoke was coming out of the chimney in spite of the warmth of the day - for the cooking, Jack explained.

The Three Men of Gragareth were prominent against the skyline, much lower down than Mike had imagined, and quite close to the farmhouse. They could see Birkwith pushing his bicycle up one of the steeper stretches of the lane opposite, "One hour to go up, five minutes to come down," Jack remarked.

Mike made a rough sketch of the area opposite, "There's plenty of cover over there by the Three Men, and that boundary wall on the west, that one going up and over the ridge, that could be useful." He slowly moved his field glasses across the fellside. "It all looks very quiet, but that in itself, I suppose could be unusual, at this time of day. Let's get back to the village and wait to see what Birkwith has to say."

Jack and Mike were chatting and drinking tea in Birkwith's front room when they heard the clatter of the constable's bike against the house wall and the thump of running boots on the path.

"He's back", Mrs. Birkwith informed them, somewhat unnecessarily, from the kitchen.

Birkwith burst in to the room, red-faced and wild-eyed, "There's summat going on", he burst out breathlessly. Mike put a warning finger to his lips and indicated the open door.

"Sorry, sir," the constable gasped, as he turned and closed it. He was still breathing heavily, and obviously excited. But it must have been the hair-raising bike ride down the hillside that was responsible for the constable's grotesque expression, Jack presumed. Rather like that pop-eyed hypnotic state induced by the whirling movement of the dervish.

"There's definitely summat going on, sir," he repeated, his voice sounding more composed now, and his features returning to their normal configuration. "I'm certain the Craven's are been held against their will, by three men, an' all."

"Did they suspect anything?" Mike asked sharply.

"Pretty certain they didn't, sir. But I knew there were summat wrong as soon as Hannah came to the door. She sounded jovial enough, but I could feel a sort of tension in her. I went in t'kitchen for a cup o'tea like I allus do. No sign o'Sam anywhere, but the parlour door was open a little bit," he showed them how much with his hands. "Hannah gave me a warning look towards it when she had her back to it, so I reckon they were hiding in there. I didn't let on anything was unusual, just asked where Sam was. She said he was out working in the barn at the back. She's a bright lass, is Hannah. When she gave me my tea she said, 'there's yer sugar, Jim, three lumps, isn't it?" He looked first at Mike, apparently expecting some comment, when that failed to materialise he turned to Jack and repeated, "Three lumps! Don't you see?"

Jack felt obliged to hazard a guess, "Three people?"

"Right. You see I don't take sugar", he said emphatically. He seemed to swell with pride as he went on, "Hannah knows that 'cos we have a little joke about it, I allus say I'm sweet enough already."

Jack sighed imperceptibly and Mike smiled, "Very well done, constable. Did you manage to get out all right?"

"No trouble, sir. We just chatted a bit about the weather and things in general, and then I said I had to call on Frank Moss down at Low Beck Farm, and left." He sat back in his chair with a satisfied look on his face. "I'm sure she knew I'd got the message though, sir," he added, as a concluding remark.

"Good," said Mike. "That's an excellent piece of work. Right, we need to get the car up here. Can I use your telephone, constable, please?"

"Of course, sir, help yourself."

Mike spoke briefly to Bainbridge at the railway station in Langham, and replaced the receiver in the cradle.

"Right, the reinforcements have arrived and I've asked PC Bainbridge to bring five of them over here straight away." He spread the map out on the table in front of Birkwith. "Now, constable, I'm leaving you in charge of this section and this is what I want you to do. He carefully outlined his plan for the capture of the farm and the apprehension of the intruders. Birkwith made laborious reminders in his notebook whilst Mike was speaking. When he had finished, Mike went over it all again and stressed the importance of the fact that no attempt at capture should be made until the lights had been lit and the aeroplane had passed overhead.

"Very good, sir. I've got all that."

"I'm relying totally on your common-sense, Constable Birkwith. We're dealing with dangerous men, and I don't want you to take any unnecessary risks."

"Thank you, sir. I know what's needed. Don't forget, sir, these are not just hostages, they're close friends o' mine."

Bainbridge arrived shortly afterwards. At Mike's request he had changed out of his uniform and his large figure looked uncomfortably constricted in his best tweed jacket.

The sergeant-in-charge and the extra men tumbled out of the close confinement of the car with vociferous expressions of delight and with a good deal of groaning and stretching, until Sergeant Mann, something of a martinet by the sound of it, told them in no uncertain terms to shut up.

Birkwith had organised his wife to make some more tea and he had arranged some extra seating in the room. After the introductions Mike briefly outlined the position in general terms and left Birkwith to fill in the details of their particular operation later. Bainbridge had brought half a dozen .303 rifles and a box of ammunition with him, and before they left, Mike instructed Birkwith to smuggle them from the car boot into the house wrapped in a blanket, to avoid any possibility of panic in the village. Although any casual glance into the Birkwiths' parlour that afternoon, and the sight of six burly plainclothes policemen squashed against the walls, with .303 rifles between their knees, would have sent tremors of fear throughout the local population within minutes.

Twelve

Kingsdale, Yorkshire Dales, 7th July 1939

Jack, Bainbridge, Sergeant Mann and with Mike at the wheel, were soon speeding down the main road towards Kingsdale. The object of this trip was to recce the area where they assumed the second signalling point would be. The Rover struggled, in spite of its 14hp engine, as it made its way up the incline out of the village of Morton towards the higher fells. After some more minutes of low gear work Mike pulled the car into the side of the road just below the brow of the hill.

"We'll get out here and walk the rest," he informed Bob. "I want you to drive back down to Morton and then along the main road and up this lane here," he indicated the place on the open map.

"Oddie's Lane, that, Inspector, bit of an old Roman road," Bob responded. "I know it well, there's some farmhouses at the top. I can wait there."

"Right, well keep your eyes open, Bob, you know what's happened in the other valley. We're going to walk along this track here, right in front of this escarpment, probably have a quick look on top if it's all clear," Mike explained.

By the time Bainbridge had turned the car round the three men had already crested the hill and the broad U-shaped valley of Kingsdale was opening up before them.

"Wow, look at that!" exclaimed Mike in awe. "What a tremendous view." The morning sunlight heightened the green of the dale and whitened the limestone outcrops on the ridges. On the left were the craggy scars below the ridge of Gragareth, matched on the right side of the valley by the similar outcrops of Ewes Top and Twistleton Scars. The narrow road, with its attendant stream in the valley bottom, stretched away into the haze of the morning. One solitary farmhouse, about a mile down on the right, was the only visible sign of habitation.

"Lovely, isn't it? One of my favourite views, this," said Jack.

"It's magnificent," murmured Mike. The three men had paused by a wall at the top of the hill and Jack pointed out the salient features regarding the signal locations.

"This is going to be your problem, Sergeant Mann," said Mike, "taking care of the group on that ridge over there." He pointed over to his right in the direction of Ewes Cross. "There'll be at least two men, but there could be more." Partially opening his map out on his knee he showed Mann the position. "We're here now," he said, "and we're going to follow this track here. However, I suggest that this evening we bring you up to this point over here, where we'll be meeting PC Bainbridge later on. You can work your way up through these crags then, should be plenty of cover for you there."

"Right, sir, that seems straight forward enough." He looked over the valley to confirm the positions. "That's the track across the front of those cliffs there, isn't it?"

Mike nodded, "Yes, we're going along there now, and we'll try and get a look over the top so you'll know what ground conditions to expect up there. We expect the signal point to be located somewhere on this 140 degree line which I've marked in here." His finger traced the pencil line across the map.

"And you say there's plenty of cover up there?" Mann enquired.

"Plenty," Jack butted in. "There's that many standing stones, stone circles, cairns, and shelters, it's like Stonehenge up there."

The other men laughed, and Jack went on, "I think they'll probably be using one of the tall cairns overlooking the valley to the right, they're ready-made signalling points."

The men strolled down the road to the valley bottom, crossed the wooden bridge over the stream and followed the walled track along the foot of the scars. To any observer they would be taken for a trio of ramblers enjoying a day out in the Dales. They were all wearing strong hiking boots and Mike had a rucksack on his back. Sergeant Mann sported a grey Harris Tweed jacket and matching flat cap which gave him a distinct county look. If he'd been wearing a cravate he could have just stepped out of a gentlemen's outfitters window in Harrogate's main street.

They reached the edge of the limestone scars, and seeing no sign of anyone about, Jack led the way up through the crag to a more elevated position. Crouching in a gryke in the limestone pavement the three men looked out over the landscape in front of them.

"It's like being on the moon, isn't it?" Mike said.

There was a distinctly unearthly look about the place, the others admitted, with the brightness of the limestone contrasting starkly with the patches of green turf between them. Jack pointed out the large cairn on the edge of the cliff and a large solitary boulder in the middle of the limestone pavement, both of which he thought were possible sites for the signals.

Mike was studying one of the old shelters through his field glasses, "I don't think that one's being used," he said after a minute's scrutiny. "It's too near the track for one thing, and a bit too obvious, for another."

On their right the dark scowling face of Ingleborough dominated the scene. The sheer cliff faces of the western approach were clearly visible, even in the shadow; its name, Black Shiver, seemed to aptly express the feelings of the observers that morning. It presented a truly formidable sight, and Mike expressed the thoughts of the three men exactly when he murmured, "Well, I wouldn't fancy trying to land an aeroplane up there, that's for sure. The pilot's certainly not short of guts."

To their left the higher ridge of Gragareth was bathed in morning sunlight and Jack drew his companion's attention to a couple of cairns on the nearside edge, which he thought would probably be on the flight path across.

Mike trained his glasses on the spot and Mann borrowed Jack's pair, and they both spent a few more moments familiarising themselves with the area.

"Apart from a few sheep, there's nothing moving at all today, except us." Mike commented. "Although I didn't expect to see any of them," he added. " They're too professional for that, it's not as if they'd have their washing on the line, or be sitting round a campfire frying Frankfurters." The other men smiled, and Jack said, "No, from what I saw last night they'll only come out at the last minute, and they're so well organised they can set it up in no time."

"And you let them do just that, Sergeant," Mike instructed. "Then when the plane's gone over the top, you and your men move in and grab them."

"Right, sir, I've got that. We can probably lie up over there in those rocks near the edge of that valley." He pointed towards the Twistleton Scars on their right.

"Yes, that seems fine, but we'll get you in position early this evening and you can decide then. I think we've seen enough now, let's get back down again."

They retraced their steps to the main track and it was not long before they came to the metalled lane and caught sight of Bob Bainbridge in the distance leaning against the bonnet of the car. The constable knocked out the dottle from his pipe when he saw them approaching and moved forward to meet them.

"Everything all right, Inspector?" he enquired earnestly, his eyes expressing his concern.

Mike quickly reassured him, and explained where they had been and the probable line of approach for Mann's group later that day. "I'll want you to bring Sergeant Mann's group up here later on, Bob, if you don't mind," he added.

Bainbridge nodded his assent, "Right sir, that'll be no problem."

"Now let's get back to the station and get the other chaps briefed and organised. They'll be wondering what the hell's going on," Mike said.

"Aye, they were doing a fair bit o' chuntering when I left 'em," commented Bainbridge with a smile.

"Were they indeed?" queried Sergeant Mann. "I'll soon sort them out," he snapped.

Twenty minutes later Mike parked the car behind the railway station in Langham. He knocked on the door and, followed by his three companions, entered the stationmaster's tiny office. Harold Winterburn was seated at his desk and his round face lit up with delight when he recognised Jack and Bob. He took off his spectacles and shook hands with Mike as Bob introduced him.

"It's like Bank Holiday Monday here today," he said cheerfully. He was enjoying this diversion from the usual mundane duties of stationmaster. "I've put your men in the waiting room, Inspector. I've closed it to the general public until further notice."

Mike apologised for all the inconvenience and thanked him for his assistance. "Without your help, Mr. Winterburn, we couldn't manage this operation. I'm sorry I can't let you know what it's about just now, but believe me, it is of the greatest national importance and, of course, must be kept absolutely secret. I think I can rely on your discretion, Mr. Winterburn."

The Stationmaster's eyes had rounded in wonder at the mention of 'national importance' and he visibly puffed with pride. He already had the best kept station on the LMS line and now national importance. "What else do you want me to do now, sir?" he asked deferentially.

"Well, if you'll excuse us now, we're going to talk to the men in the waiting room. I'd just ask you to keep people away from that part of the platform, if you would, but without raising any suspicions."

"Leave it to me, Inspector," he buttoned up his uniform, held open the door for them and followed them onto the platform.

The five policemen in the waiting room hurriedly straightened themselves when they saw their sergeant passing the window, and when he came in with Mike and the others, the silent apprehensive atmosphere reminded Jack of a dentist's waiting room.

After the introductions Mike explained the whole operation to them. He explained, with the help of a map on the wall, where their colleagues were and what they would be doing, the risks involved and the type of people they were dealing with. He apologised for keeping them here but explained how important secrecy was for the success of their mission. Jack could see that Mike, by being completely frank with the men, had gained their respect immediately. He dealt fully with each area of operation and the allocation of men to each. Mike asked the sergeant for the names of the men he'd left in Beckley and jotted them down in his notebook. "Beck Fell party, signal one, under the command of Jim Beckwith," he announced, and read out the names of the five constables. "Scales Moor party, signal two, Sergeant Mann, and four men from this group. He wrote down the names of the first four from the right, smiled at the fifth one and said to him, "I'm sorry about this, constable, but you'll be with me. You can see we're a bit short staffed, to put it mildly. Your name is?"

The young constable grinned, "Bridges, sir. It's all right with me sir. I see enough of this lot at work."

There was some light-hearted banter at the remark and Mike laughed along with them. "So, gentlemen," Mike cut the chatter short, "Ingleborough party, myself, Jack, Constables Bainbridge and Bridges."

God, thought Jack, we'll be a bit thin on the ground, won't we? He caught Mike's eye and knew instinctively that the very same thought was in his mind too, and he added, in reply to Jack's unspoken question, "If I can get any more reinforcements before we start I will do, of course. But I think groups one and two will be able to manage, at a pinch. A territorial army unit is supposed to be sending some men up from Skipton, but I've not heard anything from them today.

Throughout the whole time of Mike's briefing the upper part of the stationmaster's figure had passed the window at regular intervals as he strutted up and down the platform with measured, self-important strides. His demeanour seeming to suggest that the security of the nation couldn't be in better hands.

A commotion outside on the platform drew the attention of the men in the waiting room. The stationmaster's raised voice could be heard remonstrating with some poor unseen member of the public, "You can't go along there, sir. No, sir. Definitely not, sir! I'm sorry, the nearest public toilet is in the village, or you might try The Flying Dutchman across the road?"

Mike smiled wryly and turned to face the men, "Right Sergeant Mann," he began. "I think .." his sentence remained unfinished because of the ringing sound of marching army boots echoing along the platform. Mike leapt to his feet, "Good God!" he shouted. He rushed out of the door and came face to face with a young subaltern, immaculately turned-out in full army uniform, complete with Sam Browne belt across his chest and holstered revolver at his side.

"For God's sake man, keep it quiet!", he cried as he swept the bewildered officer into the stationmaster's office.

"I'm sorry," Mike apologised to the flustered man, but secrecy is essential at the moment. No one must know you're here. I'm Inspector Bannerman, by the way." Mike now had a good look at the young man for the first time. Age; not much more than twenty, Mike guessed. Slim build, rosy complexion, probably public school cadet force experience. His face had a smooth blandness to it, as yet unlined by any of life's worries.

"Second Lieutenant Nigel Percival, 1st Battalion T.A. West Yorkshire Regiment, sir," he said in light treble voice. " Sorry, sir, we've been rushing about all day to get here, we didn't get the orders until this morning."

"Look, Percival, you don't know how glad I am to see you, I was getting worried. Now, how many men have you got?"

"Ten men, one sergeant and myself, sir." he said formally, standing to attention.

"All right, relax Mr. Percival, what transport?"

"One 15 cwt truck and one GPV Sir."

"What in God's name is a GPV?" Mike asked.

"General Purpose Vehicle, sir. It's a prototype, American, I think. We're doing some secret test trials for them in this country, sir", Percival explained.

"What is it then? Some kind of tank?"

"Not exactly, sir, it's a 4x4 5cwt. command reconnaissance vehicle. The transmission can drive all four wheels, it can go anywhere, sir, cope with rough terrain, muddy ground, steep hills. My uncle, Brigadier Marston-Shepppley, do you know him, sir?" Mike shook his head, a wry smile forming at the corner of his mouth.

"Well," Percival went on guilelessly. " He has a lot of connections in the motor car industry, and he thought it'd be jolly useful up here."

"Indeed, it will," agreed Mike. "Well done, Percival, I'm looking forward to seeing what it can do. Now, what weapons have you got with you?"

"Each man has his .303 Lee Enfield, the sergeant has a .38 Webley, and I've got this special .45 Webley. "He drew the revolver from its holster. "It was a twenty-first birthday present from my unc...."

"All right, Percival." Mike butted in sharply, put it away there's a good chap. What else have you got?"

"We've got an LMG, that's a bren gun," he added didactically. Mike raised his eyebrows ever so slightly. "And I've a box of grenades, some boxes of ammo, and K rations for twelve."

"That's excellent. What I want you to do now is to get your vehicles out of sight round the back. Keep your men there for the time being until I make space for them in the waiting room."

"Will do, sir," He drew himself up and appeared to be about to salute and stamp his feet, but seeing the look in Mike's eyes, decided otherwise and backed apologetically out of the office.

Mike returned to the waiting room and told the others about the reinforcements. "I'm afraid I won't be needing you with us now, Constable Bridges," he said with a grin. "It's back with Sergeant Mann and your colleagues in group two for you. Sorry about that," he added, as a look of mock anguish flashed across the constable's face.

"There will be two men here in reserve, with a vehicle, at all times. I shall be taking seven soldiers with me in my group. We'll be splitting into two groups later on," he explained. "And I've decided to put a small unit on the road at the top of the hill overlooking Kingsdale, that's where we started walking this morning, Sergeant Mann." He looked at Mann, who nodded his head. "They will be there as reinforcements for you if you need them, and also to pick up anyone who might be trying to escape down that valley from either ridge." He pointed out on the map where exactly the unit would be and how its position fitted in with the rest of the operation.

When Mike had finished the whole group trooped out to the car park at the back of the building to sort out their rations and ammunition. As they rounded the corner they were faced with a most peculiar looking vehicle. It looked like a square tin box on wheels, it had no roof and just a rudimentary windshield to protect the passengers from the elements.

"What the bloody hell is that?".

"Mobile sardine tin, if you ask me."

"Tin can on wheels," and other disparaging comments were bandied about, until Mann called them to order.

Mike told them what little he knew about the GPV and concluded by telling them that, in first gear, it was capable of going up the back wall of the railway station.

This stretched their credibility to some extent but they crowded round the vehicle with great interest, whilst the driver, a dark haired man with a pencil moustache, ignored their attentions, and sat nonchalantly cleaning his finger nails, occasionally glancing at his reflection in the rear view mirror and smoothing down the sides of his glossy black hair with his hands.

Now that Mike had the use of the army truck he had decided to let Mann take the Rover up Oddie's Lane to the edge of the fell, and keep it there for the return. He suggested to the sergeant that he let his group relax in the sun for the rest of the day and only move them up into the forward positions at the last minute. They waved farewell to the men as the black Rover, loaded to the gunnels, lumbered out of the car park and headed for the main road.

"That's another group organised," Mike muttered to Jack. "Two down, one to go. Let's get this lot inside."

Yet again Mike went over the operation. Jack couldn't help noticing that the outline had got shorter, and the delivery slicker. Mike must have also been aware of this, and also the inherent danger of under-informed personnel, because at one stage he asked Bob Bainbridge to take over. The latter's slow pedestrian briefing was in complete contrast to Mike's style but it served it's purpose admirably and the soldiers were meticulously taken through each stage of the operation. Mike only stepped in at the end to explain the soldiers' own particular role. He assigned Lieutenant Percival and two men to the road-block on the Kingsdale road, stressing the strategic importance of the position, yet privately feeling that he would be well out of harm's way there. He asked Percival to allocate two men to stay in reserve at the station with the GPV and the remaining seven to accompany himself, Jack and Bainbridge. Mike then showed them on the map the position at the bottom of Long Lane where he wanted the 15cwt truck during the operation.

Jack could appreciate the thinking behind this, because Long Lane was the green road which ran in a straight line for about a mile and a half along the opposite side of the valley to his uncle's farm; it was a quick, albeit very rough, connecting route between the village and the open moor near Bar Pot.

Mike was eager to get the soldiers out of the village as soon as possible. It only needed one of Bergman's men to get a glimpse of the soldiers for the whole operation to be ruined. Bergman's men could disappear into the countryside without a trace, and the lives of the hostages would be at risk. These thoughts were in Mike's mind as he hustled Percival and his two men into the GPV and sent them off up the lane, with Bob Bainbridge pedalling in front of them on his bicycle to check that the way was clear.

"Getting more and more like Fred Karno's army every minute, is this," Mike said in some dismay.

"They'll be all right once they're on the main road and out of the way." Jack had felt the need to bolster up Mike's spirits, as he also was beginning to get very worried. You couldn't keep things quiet for long in a small village like Langham. And they seemed to have had half the British army and most of the Yorkshire Police Force pass through this morning already.

"It could have been worse, Mike," Jack added in an attempt to cheer him up. "They could have brought the military band with 'em; we might have had the massed pipes and drums marching up the main street."

Mike laughed as he imagined the situation, "Yeah, and Bergman taking the salute from the balcony of The Old Crown."

Bob Bainbridge freewheeled round the corner at that moment, his ruddy face beaming. "All right, sir, they got away all right."

"Right let's have a quiet chat, the three of us, to sort out the next stage."

They spent the next thirty minutes in the stationmaster's office going over the arrangements for the dispersal of the soldiers. Jack proposed that the best place to hold the men during the day would be up at his uncle's farm, it was the ideal place from which to move into position around Bar Pot, he told them. The truck could be kept out of sight in the big barn and the men would be contained on the farm. The strength of his argument was overwhelming and the others agreed immediately. It was possible to avoid the village main street by taking a long round about route to the farm along the back lanes, but all three agreed that it was worth the effort to reduce the risk of discovery.

The crunch of tyres on gravel attracted their attention, and glancing up they saw the head and shoulders of the driver of the GPV flash past the window towards the rear of the building. The clatter of studded army boots in the passage way and along the platform further announced the driver's arrival.

"Oh, for God's sake", Mike muttered testily. "Let's get this lot out of here. I'll go with them in the truck to show 'em the way. You cycle up to your place, Bob, and see if everything is quiet in the village, and Jack, I think you'd better get up to the farm first and warn your aunt that we're coming. Be careful and just check that there's none of their lot about. We've been a bit out of contact with them today."

The three men arranged to meet at the farm at four o'clock, which gave them just over forty minutes to make their separate ways there. When Jack and Bob had left, Mike thanked the stationmaster for his invaluable help, and arranged for the two men who were going to stay there in reserve, to be accommodated in his office near the telephone. He told the army sergeant, a veteran of the Great War, by the look of his rugged face and the row of service ribbons on his tunic, what they had decided and asked him to get the men into the truck with as little disturbance as possible.

Jack cringed at the first shout from the sergeant.

"Right you men get fell in outside! Hurry up! Come on now, move yourself, move yourself".

"Sergeant, sergeant." Mike said quietly. "Let's move them out two at a time so we're not too obvious?"

"Very good, sir," he said quietly to Mike. He turned to the men and in a voice hardly less stentorian than before shouted, "Right men, you heard the hofficer! Quiet..erly... qui..ert..erly, I said!.. in twos, to the vehicle...go!"

Mike shook his head, muttered something inaudible under his breath, and went out to the truck.

Thirteen

Langham, Yorkshire Dales, 7th July 1939

Jack observed his uncle's farm from behind the dry-stone wall for some minutes; all seemed to be in order. The smoke from the chimney was curling up into the still air, the washing was hanging limply on the line, drying in the sun today rather than in the wind as was more usual. Jack sprinted, half-doubled, across the open ground of the pasture and flattened himself against the farmhouse wall. He edged quickly to the corner of the house and looked round, ducking back hurriedly when the door latch and the door opened. He needn't have worried because on his second peep round he saw his aunt, wicker laundry basket at her feet, un-pegging clothes from the line.

Not wishing to startle the old lady Jack backed off across the field, regained the path and casually sauntered up. The dog appeared at the open door, first its ears pricked up and then it dashed towards him, its tail lashing the air as it whirled around him in a frenzied welcome.

"Hello, Aunty", he called when he was near enough. "Good drying day, isn't it?"

"Eeeh, hello Jack. It's set fair for t' next few days, they said on the wireless this morning."

"Oh, that's good news then. It'll dry the pastures out nicely."

When they were in the house Jack told her about the soldiers who were coming up. Her face took on a worried expression until Jack pointed out that they were only here on manoeuvres, but had offered to help in the search for Uncle Joss whilst they were in the vicinity. She seemed satisfied with that explanation and, in keeping with her philosophy of feeding all visitors, started making the necessary catering preparations for a group of ravenously hungry men.

At 4 o'clock Jack took up a position by the open door so that he could watch each direction. Bob Bainbridge was the first to arrive, he had walked up the track from the valley bottom and Jack saw him wipe his forehead with his handkerchief as he paused by the lower gate.

"Phew," he gasped as reached Jack, "It's a warm 'un, today, lad."

"It is that," agreed Jack. He listened intently for a moment his head cocked on one side. "That's Mike with the truck, I think, coming up the lane. I'll go and open the gate for 'em, will you just guide 'em into the barn? I've already opened the door."

The small truck swept past Jack at the gate as he waved it on to Bob, who directed it into the barn with the flourish of a professional traffic controller.

Later that afternoon in the quiet of the front bedroom Mike, Jack and Bob, pots of tea at their elbows, sat round the map on the table. They could hear the muted voices of the soldiers chatting and joking in the kitchen below as they tackled, with undisguised enthusiasm, the pyramid of sandwiches Aunt Dorcas had prepared for them. She would enjoy that as much as they did, Jack thought.

"Now," said Mike. "Bob says things seem to be quiet in the village so we're assuming everything is going on as planned. We'll know for certain when Bergman comes up that track down there like he did last night. About 7:30pm it was, so we'll be watching from, say 7:00pm onwards?" The others nodded their approval. "Right, I want you, Bob, to be in charge of this area down here." He circled the point on the map. "Take three men and conceal yourselves somewhere on the moor, well back from this Bar Pot crater to start with, you can creep up to the rim of the hollow later on when it starts to get dark. There's plenty of cover there. You'll have the Bren gun with you, if there's any trouble that'll keep their heads down. Remember there are at least four men down there, and definitely one hostage. It's a difficult job, I

126

know, but if we can take the summit party without any shooting, we can get down and back you up.

"Right you are, sir," Bainbridge acknowledged. " We won't take any action unless we're forced to. We'll just sit there and wait for you."

"That's about it, Bob. But the main thing is to keep your heads down until the plane has landed."

At the mention of the word 'hostage' Jack's mind had immediately turned to thoughts of Ruth. He'd been so involved in the events of the day he'd almost forgotten about her. A feeling of guilt crept over him as he wondered how she was coping in the confines of the cave. We've got to get her out tonight, he thought.

His thoughts were brought back to the present by the sound of his name. Mike was talking to him, "Jack, we can expect the plane to land sometime about 9:00pm, so we want to be in position on the summit by about 8:00pm, I should think."

"Yes," Jack agreed. "We ought to allow about an hour from here to get in position."

"Which is the best way for us to get up there?"

Jack went through the various possibilities, and after some discussion it was decided that the best route would be the one Jack had followed the previous evening. Other routes exposed them to a greater risk of observation, either from the summit, or the Devil's Gill area.

"All right then, that's settled. There'll be Jack, me, the army sergeant and two other men in the summit group. When everyone is out of the way the other chap can take the truck to the bottom of Long Lane and wait there in case we need transport up on the moor." Mike looked out of the window and across the valley. "That's Long Lane over there, isn't it?" He said, pointing about half way up the hillside.

Jack confirmed this and added, "It's also the way we'll be going tonight. I've been thinking, Mike, it might be better if our group goes in the truck to the bottom of the lane and walks up from there. There'd be less chance of being seen than if we crossed the valley, it's a bit exposed going across there and it'd look a bit out-of-place for so many people at that time of night."

"Good idea, we'll do that, Jack. It gives us an extra man, as well, because we can take the driver with us instead of leaving him down there at the bottom of the lane."

Mike sat back in his chair and sighed, "It's a massive operation, is this. I can't say I like it at all. It's too involved, too many chances for it to go wrong." He rested his chin on his hands and looked thoughtfully at the map again, but both Jack and Bob realised he wasn't actually seeing anything. Mike was responsible for a complex operation involving the lives of many people and he was worried about how it might turn out.

"You've done the best you can, sir," Bob said spiritedly, coming to Mike's defence. "You've only been up here a couple o' days and you've organised all this."

Mike smiled, " Yeah, thanks Bob, we had to act quickly as soon as we found out what was going on." He paused for a second, and when he spoke again a note of sincerity had come into his voice, "I'll tell you something though, gentlemen. I'm glad you and Jack are with me in this, I'd be bloody well lost without you two." He pointed to the map, "Look we're too spread out, there are one, two, three four major areas to cover; it wouldn't have be so bad if the army had brought some wireless sets with them."

"One of the chaps told me they only had two in the barracks, and neither o' them were working," Bob informed them succinctly.

"It's to be hoped we don't go to war with anybody just yet then," remarked Mike dryly.

When they returned to the kitchen, Dorcas was busy preparing packs of sandwiches for the men to take with them on their search. In response to Jack's seemingly innocuous question about any visitors she might have had recently, his aunt told him that the only people who'd been up to see her were two of her friends from the village institute. They'd strolled up that morning to bring her some home-made jam and see how she was. Jack and Mike exchanged glances, clearly relieved that the farm had received no unwelcome attention. Jack, however, with a suspicious glance at the sandwiches, just hoped that the fillings and the visitors' generosity were not connected. Jam sandwiches on a bleak mountainside could lower morale quicker than a cold shower on a winter's night.

The next half hour was spent in the barn. Weapons were checked and issued, ammunition allocated and each group briefed as to its position and involvement.

When Mike was satisfied that everybody understood what they were doing he sent them back to the farmhouse with their sergeant. Bob was looking disparagingly at the ancient rifle he was holding, "You know," he remarked with smile, "the one I had on the Somme was damn sight better than this." He opened and closed the bolt a few times, and held the barrel up to the light to look through it. "That spider's going to get a shock if I ever fire this, trouble is, I might, as well." The others laughed.

Mike slipped a couple of grenades into the pocket of his rucksack, "These might come in useful," he muttered. He delved into the main compartment of the bag and handed Jack the pistol he'd taken from Ruth's case. "You take this, Jack. It's a seven-shot Walther, there's a spare magazine here. There's the safety catch, and you load it like this," he explained, taking the gun back and demonstrating the actions. "I've got my own gun in here somewhere," and he rooted around in the rucksack again. "Ah, here it is," he said as he drew out a bulky .38 general service revolver, broke it open and checked the action. "It should be all right, I've only ever used it on the range."

Bob drew his pocket watch out and glanced at it.

"Time we were watching, Bob?" Mike enquired, raising his eyebrows.

"Just about, sir, better early than miss 'owt, I reckon."

Jack, Mike and Bob seated in the front bedroom took it in turns to watch the track below the farm. They chatted desultorily at times but these were interspersed with long periods of silence as each man was preoccupied with his own thoughts.

The valley below the farm was already in shadow and the line of demarcation between sun and shade was inching up the green slope on the opposite side. It had almost reached the level of Long Lane when Bob, on duty at the window, suddenly drew back and whispered urgently," He's here!"

"Thank God, for that," said Mike with feeling. Up to that moment he'd been becoming increasingly worried about his planning. He wriggled over to the window and cautiously peered out from behind the curtain. Bergman was strolling casually along the path, looking like a benevolent man of the cloth on his evening constitutional. The casual observer might even think he was preparing next Sunday's sermon in his head, as he stopped to examine some wild flower, or gaze across the valley with a serene expression of wonder on his face. Bergman only glanced briefly up at the farm when he reached the gate, but Mike was not taken in by this apparent indifference and kept well out of sight. Some yards farther on the parson stopped, ostensibly to fasten his shoe-lace, but Mike could see that the man's eyes were carefully scrutinising the farm under his lowered brow.

"Crafty old devil," murmured Mike, as he watched him. "Right, he's moving again." He kept his eyes on the track for a couple of minutes to make sure the parson did not reappear, then he turned to Jack and Bob, "Right, chaps, this is it. Let's get moving!"

They wished each other good luck and Bob led his group out of the back of the farm towards the open moor. The other soldiers piled in the back of the truck and Mike fastened the back cover down to conceal them, before climbing into the cab with Jack and the driver.

Fourteen

Ingleborough, Yorkshire Dales, 7th July 1939

The short drive through the upper part of the village was achieved without any awkward moments and the truck was soon lurching its way up the walled track towards Long Lane. Faced with a good hour and a half's walk in front of them Mike moved the group up the lane at a steady pace. Their movement up the lane was concealed from the valley by the limestone wall on their left, and even after they had reached the open ground beyond the top gate, the lie of the land was in their favour and kept them hidden from anyone in the Bar Pot area.

Jack led the group through the limestone escarpments, where possible on the well defined green tracks. He knew the walking and the concealment would not be as easy on the higher ground on the approach to Ingleborough. He was glad they'd had a long spell of dry weather because he knew from experience how boggy that area became after a drop of rain. Jack stopped at the top of one grassy hillock and lay down and Mike crept up to join him; together they carefully studied the area in front of them. At this point they would leave the springy short-cropped grass of the limestone pastures and move onto the rougher terrain of tufted hussocks. It was a brown trackless area dissected by a number of small streams flowing into the main water catchment area for this side of the mountain.

"We'll have to be careful crossing this bit," Mike warned. "Only one man to move at a time, move and then lie still until the next man gets to you."

"Look," interrupted Jack, nodding towards a saddle on the ridge. Two figures had appeared, clearly visible on the skyline, and heading in the direction of the summit. "That's the landing party going up."

"Good," grunted Mike. "At least we know where they are now."

They watched until the men had disappeared from view and then, moving as planned, crossed the intervening stretch of land to the opposite slope. It was a time-consuming exercise moving one at a time and the light was fading as they regrouped just below the ridge where the men had been sighted. After a few minutes rest Jack led the way over the ridge, crossed the well-defined footpath and headed for the protective cover of the summit crags. He moved slowly towards the southern rim of the summit, well away from the spot where the landing equipment was stored, and managed to find an ideal place for concealment between two large rocks.

"Hang on here a minute, while me and Jack have a quick recce," Mike ordered. The men, breathing heavily, flopped out on the grass between the rocks without a word, glad of the rest after, what for them, appeared to be unaccustomed, and particularly strenuous exercise.

Mike was impressed with the summit plateau, "Massive, isn't it?" he said, in some awe. They could see the men preparing the landing zone at the far end of the summit; from their movements it was obvious that they were working diligently and were completely absorbed in their task.

"We can move nearer by going round that side to the left, there's rocks and cover all the way round," Jack suggested.

"Yes," Mike agreed thoughtfully. "I want to be as near to the end of the landing ground as possible, so I can stop the plane taking off again if I get chance. I think it'll be best if we split the group, Jack. You take the men and go to the other side of that shelter and take them from the rear whilst they're occupied with the plane. Do you think you can get 'em across without being seen?"

"Should be all right, we can crawl across over this way. Everybody's going to be looking the other way when the plane comes in, aren't they?"

Mike agreed, "Right then, that's it. You get the ground party, I'm going to try and get the pilot; the other two will be coming up in a minute or two, won't they?" He said, glancing over his shoulder down towards the main track. "Let's get the men briefed."

He slithered down between the rocks followed by Jack and rejoined the group.

"Right chaps, listen. First of all this is a police operation, not a military one. Anytime now there will be a couple more Germans coming up. We let the plane land and then we move, and we move quickly. I know the easiest way would be to pick them off from a distance, but we're not at war with Germany and we don't want to provoke an international incident. We're here to arrest them for illegal entry, is that understood?" The men murmured their understanding. "No one opens fire unless me or Jack give the order, and that'll only be in self-defence." He looked around the group to see that his words had taken effect.

"The other two are here now, Mike," Jack muttered quietly. He had been watching the summit with his eyes at ground level whilst Mike had been speaking. The latter joined him on the rim and they watched as the two newcomers joined the landing party near the shelter. They could see the Germans checking their watches and glancing out to sea, but Jack knew it would be some time before the plane arrived. He knew it wasn't quite dark enough yet.

The evening sky was only slightly less beautiful than the previous evening, the clouds on the horizon were still tinged with a fading crimson and the sands of Morecambe Bay reflected the sky's russet sheen.

"Unreal, isn't it?" Mike muttered after some minutes of silent observation. "Unreal, and absolutely beautiful."

Shortly afterwards there was some activity amongst the landing party and the lights check started. From their position Jack and Mike were unable to see the lights on Scales Moor, but way across two valleys and the intervening ridge, the short piercing flashes of light indicated that the unit on Gragareth were ready.

"Thank God for that," said Mike. "It looks as though they've all checked out. That means nobody on our side has blown their cover. I've been worried about that all day."

The light in the sky had now faded considerably and darkness was creeping in imperceptibly from the east. An excited shout from the Germans attracted their attention and their pointing arms told them that the plane had been sighted. Mike focussed his glasses on the point, and watched it for a minute as it headed in a north-easterly direction towards Beck Fell.

"Airspeed Envoy, registered in Northern Ireland", he said authoritatively. "They can carry six passengers as well as the pilot, I hope to God it's not full. Right, Jack," he said, turning to his companion, "time you were getting your men across there. Keep your head down, and good luck".

"Aye, and the same to you," Jack replied fervently.

Fifteen

Beckley, Lancashire, 7th July 1939

The road to Beck Fell Farm, Sam and Hannah Craven's place, is a narrow metalled lane which winds its way up the right hand side of the valley from the village of Beckley, some one and half miles to the south. On the hillside behind the farm three prominent stone cairns, known locally as the Three Men of Gragareth, stand like a giant set of cricket stumps. Their commanding position on the edge of the desolate moor immediately draw the eyes of any traveller coming up the lane. Beck Fell Farm snuggles at the foot of the fell directly beneath the cairns.

In the early evening of that day PC Jim Birkwith, the village constable, had brought his group of five colleagues up to a boundary wall from which they could observe the farm without being seen. They'd spent most of the afternoon lying in the sun in Jim's back garden and drinking tea, and were eager to get on with the job. Jim, however, mindful of the Inspector's instructions, was having no foolhardy heroics, and he told them so in no uncertain terms.

"Them folk in there are friends o' mine, and we're going to get 'em out safely. We do nowt until the plane's gone over, and then we try and get the Jerries when they're up on the hillside. Got that?" The men appeared to have 'got it' so Birkwith outlined the plan he'd been carefully preparing for the last five hours. He despatched three men up the hillside away from the house and out of sight of it, to work around the ridge towards the cairns. They were to conceal themselves there until the plane had passed over and then, and only then, he stressed were they to apprehend the men on the lights.

Birkwith waited until it was almost twilight before he made his move and he and the two men with him wriggled up the side of the wall in the direction of the farm. After a short time they could move more freely as the outbuildings shielded them from the farm windows.

"Wait here", he muttered tersely to his companions, and he slithered round the side of a barn on his stomach to get a clearer view of the house. The farm looked particularly peaceful on this warm summer evening; the grey stone walls, usually harsh and weather-beaten, were softened by a warmer glow from the last rays of the setting sun.

Birkwith's eyes noted the smoke from the chimney and the drawn curtains in the downstairs rooms. The unnatural silence of the place worried him. He hoped to God nothing had happened to Sam or Hannah. What if there'd been a struggle or something like that? He forced these thoughts out of his mind and squirmed round to the back of the barn. The two men lay sprawled out on the grass in apparent contentment, as though on some Sunday outing in the country. At the sight of the disapproval on Birkwith's face they grabbed their rifles and adopted a more alert position, crouching by the side of the barn. Birkwith lay on his stomach at the corner of the building and peered through the long grass at the farmhouse.

The shadows of the farm buildings lengthened, stretched up the hillside and gradually disappeared into a grey mistiness. Birkwith had watched them, it was difficult to feel any menace or envisage any danger in such a peaceful setting and he was finding it difficult to concentrate. He yawned and stretched his legs out behind him and looked across at his colleagues propped up against the back wall of the barn. He was about to tell them it wouldn't be long now, when the sound of the farm door opening brought him to instant concentration. He waved the two policemen down and put his finger to his lips. Very slowly he raised his eyes to get a better view.

Three men had emerged from the farm and were heading across the yard in the direction of the gate which led to the hillside. They were only in sight for three or four seconds but Birkwith had immediately recognised Sam's stocky figure in the middle.

"Looks as though they've left one in the house to guard the woman," he whispered to the others. "They've taken Sam up the hillside with 'em. We don't move until the plane's gone over mind, then me and Sid are going to get up alongside the house by the door, and I want you, Stan, to get by that wall over there so you can cover the back door." The two men muttered their agreement, and Birkwith continued, "and no shooting if you can help it".

After what seemed ages, but was in fact only twenty minutes, the sound of high flying aeroplane could be heard coming up the valley. Birkwith and his men rolled onto their backs and stared up into the sky; one of them pointed and Birkwith made out the shape himself as the plane banked to its right almost overhead. "Right, here we go then, lads," he whispered as he crawled round the corner of the barn. He tip-toed across the yard to the house wall and flattened himself against it and Sid joined him shortly afterwards. They inched their way round the wall until they could see the door; a shaft of light illuminated the cobbles in the yard. Birkwith drew back quickly, "It's open. I think they're coming out," he whispered hoarsely in Sid's ear. Birkwith's second careful glance confirmed his surmise to be accurate. A man in a green uniform was now standing in the yard looking skywards in the direction the plane had taken. Hannah was standing in the doorway behind him. The full light of the lamp fell across her shoulders as she stood, arms folded, her worried face looking up into the night sky.

"Come on, Sid, let's get 'im while he's outside", Birkwith slipped the safety catch off on his rifle and stepped round the corner and moved towards the doorway, carefully placing each foot on the cobbles as quietly as possible, but never taking his eyes of the man in the yard. He could sense Sid creeping along just behind him. They were about five yards away when there was a warning bark from the dog in the house, the man whirled round; his face contorted with panic when he saw the two rifles levelled at his chest. His hand fluttered momentarily in the direction of his pocket, but the hopelessness of his situation was all too apparent, and he slowly raised his hands in the air. Birkwith quickly disarmed him and directed him into the lighted kitchen.

"Eeeh, I'm right glad to see you, Jim Birkwith," Hannah said with feeling, when the door was closed and bolted behind them. "They've got Sam up there with 'em, you know, Jim, two more of the blighters."

"Aye, I got your message, lass," he grinned. "I've got some men up there to look after that end." He looked at the prisoner, "We'd better get him tied up and gagged in case some of his pals come down looking for him." They trussed their prisoner to a chair with a length of washing line and tied one of Sam's woolly scarves around his head and carried him into the darkened parlour. "You stay here with him, Sid, for a minute. Keep a watch out of that window as well. I'm just going to tell Stan what's been going on."

When Birkwith returned Hannah had a pot of tea ready for him which he accepted gratefully, "Thanks, love, that's just what I needed." He beckoned Sid in from the parlour to get his tea, "Hannah, I want you to watch that chap in there if you will, love, while we just get ready in here in case they come back".

He lit the paraffin lamp in the parlour, drew the curtains and closed the door. Then he extinguished the lamp in the kitchen and he and Sid took up a position at each of the windows, overlooking the cobbled yard.

They had only just settled into position when the silence of the night was shattered by a staccato volley of gunshots from the fellside above them. Hannah's anxious face appeared at the door behind them. "It's all right, love. Them's our men firing up there. They'll be down in a minute, just you watch that fellow in there." He sounded considerably more confident than he felt and he gripped his rifle tighter, cocked the gun and eased off the safety catch. Glancing across the room at Sid, he shrugged his shoulders and muttered, "I hope to God it was our men, I wish I knew what was going on."

He didn't have long to wait. A flickering line of slow moving lights was coming down the hillside towards the farm. "Let 'em come through the door, well take 'em by surprise if we can," Birkwith said steadily.

The descending lights were no longer visible now. It seemed to Birkwith, peering out into the shadows of the outbuildings, that the men were regrouping by the gate in the perimeter wall.

At the other window Sid tensed and raised his rifle, "On the right," he called tersely.

Birkwith glanced across the yard, "Hold it, Sid!" he shouted with relief, "It's Stan", he added, as he spotted the policeman he'd left on guard. As the constable got nearer the door Birkwith could see the wide smile on the man's face and his 'thumb's up' sign.

The group of men appeared in view and Birkwith recognised Sam and two of the policemen. He undid the bolts, flung open the door and rushed out into the yard to greet them.

"Everything all right?" he shouted excitedly. "We heard the shots down here."

"Burns got hit," said one constable. "Not seriously, though" he added quickly. "One o' them's dead, unfortunately. The other's here, Bill's keeping an eye on 'im."

"Are you all right, Sam?" Birkwith asked. "Yer missus is in the house worried sick about yer."

"I'm champion now, Jim. You men have done a reet good job. I'm proud of you. Come in, all of you".

From outside in the yard Birkwith could hear Hannah's cry of delight and her emotional greeting as she embraced her husband. Round the kitchen table over a pot of tea Jim Birkwith listened intently as Bert Fielder, self-appointed spokesman for the group, recounted what had happened at the cairns. "We got up there early and took up positions in a half-circle like, a bit higher up than the Three Men. There were plenty of sink holes up there so we was well hidden. Just before it got dark two Jerries came up with Mr. Craven here, and set up three lamps on the cairns. After about ten minutes or so the plane went over. Mr. Craven was sat on a rock about ten yards in front of me. The trouble started when we heard some shooting further up the hill. One of the Jerries pulled his gun out and pointed it at Mr. Craven. He dived backwards out of the way and the Jerry fired at him. I let the Jerry have it and he fell back against one of the cairns, the other one started firing at me and then all the rest joined in and killed him straight off." The policeman paused while he organised his recollection of the events.

"Oh yeah, that's the chap I hit in the shoulder," he continued pointing to the German soldier groaning on the settee. "We left the body of the other one up by the cairns 'cos we didn't know what was going on down here till we met Stan at the gate."

"Well done, all of you," said Birkwith, the pride and relief difficult to keep out of his voice. "You've done a marvellous job."

"They have that," Sam concurred. "We're grateful to 'em, aren't we, love?" Hannah's gratitude was all too obvious in her face, and words were not necessary.

"I'm going down to the village in a minute to fix some transport for the prisoners and the wounded. Some of us'll have to stay here tonight, I'm afraid. We don't know what's happened up on the ridge yet, you see."

"You can all stay if you want," Hannah butted in. "The least we can do for you is put you up and feed you."

Before he left Birkwith organised a roster for outside guard duty. He didn't intend his group to be caught unawares by any Jerries coming down their side of the ridge. It was with a light heart that Jim Birkwith strode down the moonlit lane towards the village. He felt a considerable pride in his achievement, he'd carried out the inspector's instructions to the letter. He'd been worried all the time about something going wrong with his part of the operation, and now it was finished. He could taste the relief. If his dignity would have allowed it, he could have danced down the lane that night. But, he thought, prospective sergeants in the police force just don't do that sort of thing.

Sixteen

Kingsdale, Yorkshire Dales, 7ᵗʰ July 1939

Second Lieutenant Nigel Percival and his two men were comfortably ensconced in the corner of a sheep-fold at the top of the road which descended into Kingsdale. Leaning against the wall, Percival scanned the surrounding area with his field glasses. To the subaltern's right the flat summit of Ingleborough was just visible over the limestone outcrops of Ewes Cross; to his left massive crags were casting long shadows down the valley towards him.

"Grub up, sir!", called one of the soldiers from a squatting position on a spread-out groundsheet.

"Thank you, Perkins," murmured Percival, still absorbed in his observations. When he was completely satisfied that all was clear he joined the men by the groundsheet.

"Ah, good man," he exclaimed as he collected his sandwich and mess tin of tea. He settled down with his back to the wall; roughing it with the men, he thought, that's the way to get their respect. At his first sip of tea he let out a high-pitched squeal of pain and dropped the mess tin onto his knees. He howled again as the hot liquid soaked through his trousers. He struggled to his feet, holding his burning mouth with one hand and attempting to pull the hot trousers away from his crotch with the other.

The two soldiers exchanged meaningful glances and sniggered into their chests. They'd met chaps like him in France in 1916, fresh-faced youths from public schools, 'born leaders of men' supposedly. A pity they didn't have the necessary life experience to do it effectively. And, in the front-line trenches, with a life expectancy of perhaps twenty minutes, they never really had much chance of getting any.

"My God!" exclaimed Percival, when he'd recovered sufficiently to be able to talk, "that was damned hot."

The next two hours were spent in somnolent ease. When the soldiers were not on watch by the wall they dozed on the groundsheet, or sat chatting and smoking together, keeping a physical, as well as a social, distance from the young officer.

Apart from the bleat of a sheep higher up the slope, or the call of a passing curlew, there wasn't a sound in the valley. The air was still and warm and the men dozed on the groundsheet, a trusting innocence on their faces, Percival thought, as he looked at them. My men. Men under my command, that had a better ring to it. He would have preferred a more active role in this campaign, but just having been newly commissioned, he felt it unwise to protest too much. He glanced at his wristlet watch, "Private Thomas!", he shouted. "You're on guard now, we'll do half an hour each from now on. Carry on."

Percival was lying on his back looking up at the sky and thinking about the Fearnley Hunt Ball at the weekend. His thoughts were on what he should wear. Should I stick with the khaki, or wear my dress uniform? I'd cut a real dash in that, he mused.

"Sir!" came the urgent call from the man on watch.

"What is it now, man?" he snapped, brutally yanked back from the arms of Lady Caroline Wentworth's adorable daughter, Bunty. It was the second time that clod Thomas had interrupted his reverie, the first, 'a man with a gun crouching by a rock, sir!', had turned out to be another rock when he'd focussed his field glasses on 'him'.

"Up there, sir," he pointed up the hillside to his front left, "in those rocks, someone moved. I'm sure of it, sir."

Percival trained his glasses in that direction for some seconds but saw nothing. "Oh, come now, Thomas. You're seeing things again, man."

"I'm not, sir." he insisted indignantly. "Look, if you don't believe me, there he is again". This time he pointed farther over to the right.

"By God, you're right, man," exclaimed Percival as his glasses picked out the green clad figure moving rapidly amongst the rocks. "Well done, Thomas."

Turning his head towards the groundsheet he called out excitedly, "Perkins! Get over here, come on man, move yourself", as Perkins seemed reluctant to make the effort. "Suspicious character on the hillside, up there, two o'clock" the young officer pointed to the spot where they'd last seen him. "He's gone now."

Percival opened his map case and extracted the neatly folded map of the area and placed it on the ground sheet. "Look here, men. This is where we are now and this is where we sighted the intruder." His well manicured forefingers indicated the relevant points. "This is what we're going to do now. Perkins?"

"Sir?"

"You will stay here on guard. Stop and question anyone coming up this road. If you have doubts about them, keep them here until I get back".

"But, sir?"

"No buts, man, you do as you're told". Percival turned his attention to the other man, "Now, Thomas, you come with me. We're going up to the ridge to reconnoitre the area, we'll try and see what that johnny's up to."

"He might be one of us?" butted in Perkins helpfully.

"We don't have any men on this side of the ridge," retorted Percival contemptuously, "and certainly not in green uniforms." Perkins muttered something under his breath, and moved over to the gate in the wall to take up his guard duties. His lips still appeared to be moving, several minutes later, as though reciting some personal litany, or even a favourite passage from King's Regulations.

"Get your pack and rifle, Thomas", Percival ordered. "Let's get moving." He carefully folded the map and placed it so he could see the relevant section through the cellophane cover of the map case, and slung it over his shoulder.

"Right", he shouted, to include both men in his instruction, "Let's synchronise our watches," he glanced down at his own wrist. His men looked at each other in bewilderment; baffled, in the first instance, by the word 'synchronise' and secondly, by the phrase 'our watches'. 'Let's' they could cope with.

"Oh, never mind," Percival muttered impatiently, seeing the bemused look on their faces. "The aeroplane's due in about three quarters of an hour, we'll be back by then."

"Come on, Thomas", Percival drew his revolver from its holster and checked the mechanism, then, carrying the gun in his right hand, the white braided lanyard snaking below his elbow, he set off up the hillside.

Percival set a quick pace, his object was to get to the nearest outcrop as soon as possible to use the cover to conceal their approach. He soon outdistanced his companion, who, being fifteen years older and nearly ten stones heavier found the climbing exacting, to say the least. At one stage Percival waited but, as soon as the gasping red-faced soldier arrived and flopped down on the grass, the 2nd lieutenant was on his feet and moving again. "Come on, man. Keep going," he urged. "We don't want to lose him." He was beginning to enjoy this, the thrill of the chase; it was like those ACC exercises they'd had on the moors, Red Army versus Blue Army.

Private Thomas 320, however, didn't appear to share his officer's enthusiasm for the chase, "Bloody 'ell", he groaned. "Just my flaming luck to get a fit young bugger like 'im." He started up the hill in Percival's wake, sweat streaming down his brow and his sodden shirt sticking unpleasantly to his back.

144

Perkins had watched their progress up the fellside with dispassionate interest, his mouth still mumbling some inexpressible inner emotions. When his comrades disappeared from sight behind the crags he spat over the wall into the road and returned to his duty.

It was a good thirty minutes before Percival actually reached the ridge, there were rather more intermediate shoulders than the young officer had calculated. He lay on his stomach and looked across a flat area of open land; from his map he worked out that the well-defined track across his front must be the Turbary Road, and the high ground behind it, Gragareth. He scanned the ground in front through his glasses; all clear, no sign of their quarry. He looked behind, no sign of his companion either. Some time later, a long time later, thought Percival, anxious to get moving before it got too dark to see, the thrutching of scrabbling feet and a stentorian gasping for breath announced Thomas's imminent approach.

"Now Thomas," he started as soon as the latter had slumped down beside him. "We've got to move quickly across this open ground, get on that track and head for that wall over there." His arm indicated a long wall which came down from the higher ridge and crossed the track at right angles. "There's nobody about and we can get some cover there, right?"

Thomas nodded his head, he hadn't the breath to speak. Anyway, he hadn't really been listening, his burning feet occupied his thoughts to the exclusion of anything else. He undid the lace of one army issue boot and pulled it off. "Aaaah," he sighed with relief as his foot, released from its constricted space, seemed to visibly expand before his eyes. He carefully examined the tender red weal which encircled his ankle, it looked as though someone had been trying to saw his leg off. "Bloody 'ell," he muttered. "I'd a been better off wearing me slippers."

"Right, man. Follow me, at the double!" and without looking round at Thomas, he was up on his feet and moving in a half crouching run towards the track, his revolver gripped in his right hand for all the world as if he was 'going over the top.'

"All he wants is a bloody whistle," grunted Thomas, as he struggled to get his swollen foot back into its instrument of torture.

Percival was about fifty yards in front of Thomas and increasing his distance by the yard when he stopped suddenly and looked up into the sky. Thomas, only too glad to do likewise, followed his gaze. The silent shape of the aeroplane passed swiftly overhead. Thomas dropped to his knees and stared, open-mouthed, as it appeared to hang over the dark valley for a second like an avenging angel with outstretched wings. Thomas, to whom the Angel of Mons had been a divine revelation, and was now an integral part of his psyche, stood transfixed, eyes agog, as it glided away over the next ridge.

He was brought back to reality by the sound of his leader's voice in the distance. With a groan of resentment, he tore his eyes from the sky, and lumbered after him.

Thomas, some forty yards behind, saw Percival reach the gate in the wall and look over. The moment he did so there were two bright flashes of light and a second later the distinctive crack of gunshots. Percival was thrown back several feet and lay flat on his back on the track. Thomas couldn't believe his eyes, was it something to do with the wings that had passed overhead?

A second later he felt a searing pain on the right side of his chest, his rifle dropped from his hands and he slumped to the ground. God, he'd been hit. He was amazed to see blood was seeping through the front of his battledress. They were under fire. Where from, for God's sake? He couldn't see anybody. In spite of his war service utter panic swept through him and the only thing he could think of was to get away from here. He grabbed his rifle and scrabbled backwards; there was another shot; he heard the bullet bite into the turf on his left. "Right, you bastards," he said through gritted teeth, his composure returning a bit after the initial shock, "try some o' this." He aimed his rifle in the general direction of the gate and squeezed the trigger. There was a resounding report from the .303 and Thomas shouted in agony as the kick of the recoil jarred his injured chest. "Oh, bloody hell," he groaned, as two more shots flew over his head. He fired at the gate again without bringing the rifle up to his shoulder, and immediately wriggled backwards and rolled over several times. Thank God, it was just about dark now, he thought, as he continued to drag his way backwards to the rocks on the edge of the slope. His chest was throbbing painfully and he tried to stem the bleeding by padding the wound with his handkerchief under his tunic. He didn't know how long he wriggled backwards before he found a gap in the crags and slithered down; he didn't seem to be able to focus his eyes properly, thankfully his chest wasn't hurting as much. He closed his eyes; if he kept still they might not find him down here.

Perkins, leaning against the wall in the lane, gave a start, he'd been daydreaming about telling the barmaid in his local pub how they'd captured the German plane - what the hell was that? Sounded like shots from up there. God, there it was again. Definitely shots. Oh God, it must be Percival and Thomas. What if they've been killed? He looked round vainly for assistance, but this only highlighted his sense of isolation and vulnerability. Perkins' thoughts swung wildly and uncontrollably between despair and hope. I'll bet they've copped that chap up there, that's it. They'll be bringing him down in a minute. These self-comforting thoughts eased his mind slightly but didn't completely stifle the gnawing, nagging doubt that all was not well.

Anyway, he thought, I'm not going up there to find out, not in the dark anyway. Blow that for a lark. My orders are to stay here and guard this post, and that's just what I'm going to do. His mind felt considerably easier after this line of thought; after all, decision making wasn't his job, that's what the officers got paid for.

Meanwhile on the ridge above, the lifeless body of Second Lieutenant Percival TA lay supine on the grass, new revolver, unfired, clutched firmly in his right hand.

Brendan O'Brady, Irish patriot, former field commander in the IRA and ruthless killer never missed a chance to strike a blow for freedom, especially a gift in the form of a British officer in full uniform. O'Brady knew there was no immediate danger from the other two soldiers, he'd been watching them for the past hour. The fact that the authorities knew something about their operation had caused him sufficient worry and he was in no doubt that the time had come to carry out the contingency plan.

He hurried back to the base camp in the cave where he and his German accomplice were holding the elderly farmer prisoner.

Seventeen

Kingsdale, Yorkshire Dales, 7ᵗʰ July 1939

Joss's routine as a captive in the cave had followed a regular pattern for the last few days. He had been allowed out of the cave during the day under close supervision. Occasionally he and one of the men would walk along the track for some exercise, but much of the time he just sat in the sunshine and thought about the farm and his life at home, and having a pint with his pals in the pub. At night one his ankles was shackled to a ring bolt in the cave floor, this was not as medievally primitive as it sounds, the bolt could have been at head height, Joss thought, but it did nevertheless ensure his continued presence the following morning. He'd been well fed and treated courteously enough but, apart from the Irishman, the others didn't bother with him very much.

It was the longest period of inactivity Joss had ever experienced and, whilst lying on the rocks in the hot sunshine with the soothing sound of a rippling stream in the background might appear an idyllic lifestyle to many people, Joss found his helplessness in the situation almost unbearably frustrating. Had it not been for the threats levelled against his wife he would have made a break for it long ago.

There'd been a bit of a panic yesterday when a man had been spotted coming along the track towards them. Joss had been hurriedly bundled into the cave and a pistol held to his head. He'd heard snatches of conversation and a dog bark and he'd guessed the person was Sam Craven from over at Beck Fell Farm. He just prayed that Sam had been suspicious enough to tell somebody what he'd seen.

Joss was not allowed outside for the rest of that morning and when he eventually was, he noticed that two of his abductors had disappeared.

Only the Irishman and one German remained; and it was obvious that they were both in excellent spirits. Everything must be going well, thought Joss, but the Irishman, taciturn as ever, was not inclined to satisfy Joss's curiosity. What he had said, however, had given Joss immense delight. His very words had been, "If all goes well, Mr Warrendale, you will be back on your own farm tomorrow and we'll be going on our holidays," and he'd laughed as he'd said it.

The reference was not entirely lost on Joss because over the past few days he'd heard Scotland mentioned more than once, and he'd gathered that whatever this lot were doing here, it was only a trial run for something much bigger up there and involving someone of much higher rank.

That evening the Irishman had left Joss and the German sitting on a slab of rock by the stream and headed off along the track. It was a walk he usually took at the same time every evening. Joss assumed it was some kind of patrol he went on, because he was always back within the hour and he would then have a short private discussion with the other chap, after which it was more or less bed-time. Animal-like they curled up in their cave at dusk and came out again in the daylight.

The Irishman was later than usual getting back, Joss was usually tucked up in his bed-roll by this time. He couldn't help but notice that his guard was becoming ever more anxious by the minute and kept casting frequent glances up into the sky. What happened next shook Joss to his core, it was so totally unexpected that he just stood and gaped, head in the air, as the winged shape passed silently overhead and, like a giant black bat, headed across the valley. It was a timeless moment for Joss, an even further extension to the dream-like sequence he'd been going through for the last few days.

The double crack of two shots on his right brought his mind back to earth with a shock. More shots followed, Joss's guard leapt to his feet and drew his gun and motioned Joss to keep still as he looked out of the crater across the open moor. He stayed there until the sound of running footsteps announced the Irishman's arrival. He slithered breathless down the slope. All was not well, that was obvious and Joss's heart sank, he could see from the serious expression on their faces as the two men conversed that the problem was one of extreme urgency. Joss was decidedly worried now, everything was not going according to their plan and it immediately raised questions about his own fate. His mind raced rapidly through the options open to him, should he make a dash over the moor now or wait a bit longer? Dashing over moors at his age was not one of his strong points, he decided.

That decision was taken out of his hands, however, because the Irishman crossed the stream. "We're leaving now, immediately!" Joss was informed curtly, "You will be left by the gate over there, no harm will come to you."

The Irishman hurried away into the cave and his German associate took Joss by the arm and led him over to the gate in the nearest wall. He handcuffed him unceremoniously to an iron ring in the gatepost and, without saying a word, left him there. Joss sat with his back to the stone gatepost, right arm held in the air by the handcuffs, bewildered by this rapid sequence of events. He felt he would be all right if he could just sit down for a minute or two to sort things out in his mind. "First, that aeroplane came over..." .

Eighteen

Over the Irish Sea, 7ᵗʰ July 1939

Major Dieter Brecht looked down as the Irish coastline receded from their view as he piloted the Irish registered Airspeed Envoy out over the Irish Sea towards the Isle of Man. He and his companion were dressed in one-piece beige flying suits, on top of which they wore the regulation yellow life-jacket.

They had taken-off some ten minutes earlier from an isolated field south of Enniskillin, on the border with the Republic. Brecht had taken the Envoy up to 5,000 feet over the Mountains of Mourne and they were now cruising at about 120 mph. The evening was clear and the last vestiges of sunset were still rose-tinting streamers of cirrus across the sky.

"Sehr schon, eh?" remarked Brecht to his young co-pilot.

"Ja, gar nicht, Herr Major," replied Richter politely.

This was Brecht's last trip, in future the youngster would have to do this little ferrying job. Brecht had received notice of his recall to the Fatherland only this morning. He was glad in a way, the trip itself was not difficult and after the first couple of times the landing was relatively easy. After all, he had far worse experiences when he was attached to the navy and had to land on the deck of an aircraft carrier. At least on this trip the landing strip, rough as it was, wasn't moving up and down.

Sitting in the small passenger cabin behind the aircrew were two men in civilian clothing; they were a taciturn pair who spoke neither to each other, nor to the flying crew.

Brecht didn't have much time for the likes of them. He preferred to do his fighting openly, and he had to admit, he rather liked the uniforms, the decorations, the power and the status. He was returning to take command of a squadron of BF 109s and he was already making plans, full of pleasurable anticipation, for the new promotion. First thing tomorrow he'd get his tailor to make him a new uniform, and he could do with a new pair of leather jackboots. He had a clear picture of himself, immaculately dressed, walking between the ranks of his new squadron on his first inspection. He smiled to himself with quiet satisfaction at the thought, and it was with some reluctance that he dragged his mind back to the present. He glanced at his watch, another hour or so and he would be finished and Richter could take over the job.

The sky ahead was darkening rapidly and Brecht opened the throttle to increase the airspeed. Precision timing was imperative on this run; he needed just enough light in the sky to judge the landing approach accurately.

They'd already passed to the south of the Isle of Man and were now fast approaching the muddy wastes of Morecambe Bay; the evening sky was reflecting from the damp sheen left by the ebb tide and it brought an unaccustomed beauty to the bare expanse.

Brecht nudged Richter and drew his attention to the estuary of the River Lune. Richter nodded his understanding and Brecht banked the aircraft slightly to port and followed the river up the valley. After a short time he cut the aircraft's speed and reduced altitude. He pointed to the altimeter on the control panel, the needle pointed to 3000 feet.

"Ja, Herr Major," Richter said flatly; he knew the route off by heart, Brecht had gone over it with him so many times before. He knew about the altitude, the lights, the landing speed, the weights, the sandwiches, he just wished the old sod would get off to Germany and leave him to handle things.

Brecht peered out of the starboard window until he saw what he was looking for, "Da, the three men", he pointed down and Richter leaned over and looked down, "Ja, Herr Major," he said in the same monotone.

Three green lights were clearly visible on the hillside as Brecht banked the aeroplane to starboard and cut the engine as he passed over them. He mimed the switching off routine to his co-pilot and Richter smiled, somewhat bleakly, and nodded. The cessation of engine noise was quite dramatic and the rush of the wind over the wings created an acute sense of unreality about the flight. Brecht could feel the nervous tension of the passengers behind him as they shuffled uneasily in their seats. He smiled to himself and thought, just wait until they see the landing ground!

The aeroplane passed over the first valley and Brecht could see two green lights on the next ridge. He checked the altimeter and made a slight adjustment to his course and headed for the massive bulk of Ingleborough looming ahead. The passengers had fleeting glimpses of rocky outcrops, dark valleys threaded with thin silver ribbons of water and broad sheets of white rock. Then the engine burst into life with an ear-shattering roar that had them grabbing their arm-rests in terror. Brecht enjoyed that bit, he never informed his passengers what to expect on these trips, his orders were simply to ferry people to and fro, and that's what he did.

Brecht checked his height again, pointing out each movement to Richter, as he had done throughout the flight. 2500 feet and lining up nicely. The double lines of the landing strip were on, thank God for that. Windspeed must be all right, direction was just about perfect, Brecht's concentration was intense, as always at this point, as he lined up the aircraft for the touch down. For the first time on the flight Richter felt apprehensive, whether it was actually seeing the sheer cliff face of the mountain rushing towards him or whether the realisation that in future he would be in charge of everyone's destiny he didn't know, but something caused a sudden chill to run through his body.

Richter could see a rough cairn of stones on the port side, shadowy figures waving in the gloom and then Brecht dropped the flaps, eased up the rudder and the wheels bumped down on the rough grass. The passengers lurched in their seats at the first contact but an involuntary cry of delight went up from them as they realised they were down and safe as the plane bumped along between the row of lights. A cloud of dust enveloped the aircraft and small stones spattered the underside of the fuselage as it taxied to a halt at the end of the landing zone. Brecht always kept the engine running, he never waited around long up here. The two men in the back got up from their seats, grunted a curt 'wiedersehen' and stepped out into the night.

Brecht leaned back in his seat, unfastened his harness and stretched his arms; turning to Richter, he smiled, "The last time for me, Richter, the first for you".

"Ja, Herr Major," the young man dutifully replied, with only the slightest hardening of the eyes.

Nineteen

Langham, Yorkshire Dales, 7th July 1939

"Look, I'm bloody well fed-up of sitting here all day doing nowt. Let's get down to t'pub for quick pint. We've supped nowt but rotten railway tea for hours." The speaker, Private Eddie Crossley, was the driver of the GPV, a thin sallow faced man in his early thirties, with an Erroll Flynn moustache and glossy black hair. The latter was swept straight back and flattened, as though steam-ironed onto his head, and the parting was so straight and centrally positioned that it appeared to indicate some latent ability in draughtsmanship.

His companion, Reg Wilkins, impressionable, good-natured and very shy was two or three years younger than Eddie. Reg was full of admiration for Eddie's sophistication, his savoir faire and the tattoes on his forearm. He liked that 'Death before Dishonour' one, and Eddie said he'd take him to a chap he knew in Blackpool who could do one for him. Eddie seemed to know all the important people and where to go to get things done.

Eddie and Reg got on very well together, each apparently providing what the other needed. Reg needed a role model and Eddie needed the adulation. Eddie had promised to teach him all the wangles in army life and he knew what he was talking about; he didn't go on parades or route marches like the other men, all he did was drive around in the officer's car all day; a right cushy number.

"Come on, let's get going!" Eddie repeated.

"We shouldn't really, Eddie. We're supposed to stay here in case they need us."

"Oh, that's a laugh, that is. Need us? They've forgotten we're even here," scoffed Eddie. "How long have we bin here now? Six hours? Seven hours? Bloody 'ell, Reg. I'll bet that lot are already in the pub theirselves. What you gunna say, Reg, when your kids ask yer, 'what did you do in the army, Dad?' all you'll be able to say is, "Well, son, we drunk gallons o' weak tea in't station waiting-room once!"

Once he'd started he wasn't easily diverted and even though his colleague had renounced his token objection, Eddie still pursued his theme. He didn't believe in cracking a nut with a sledgehammer if you could use a steam-roller. "It's not as if we're proper soldiers, you know. We're not stupid regulars like that snotty 'aparth who's in charge, he knows bugger all, except what bleeding knife and fork to use in t'officers mess."

Swept out of the stationmaster's office on the tide of rhetoric Reg followed his mentor onto the platform. They were surprised to meet the stationmaster himself standing by the wrought iron gates at the entrance. Harold Winterburn had found it difficult to keep away from his office, the nerve centre of the operation, during this national emergency, and he'd popped over from his railway cottage from time to time to see if he was needed.

Eddie greeted him with a friendly wink, "Keep an ear open for the telephone, Harold, old chap, will yer? Me and Reg here have been called out on patrol. We'll not be long."

"Aye, right, 'course lads," agreed the ever eager stationmaster. "Just leave it to me." He rubbed his hands gleefully and headed for his office, or rather, the Operational HQ.

The GPV shot out of the station forecourt, turned up the lane with a screech of tyres, and within minutes was on the main road heading north.

Eddie grinned and nudged his companion, "What did I tell yer, Reg? You've just got to handle people the right way. Now let's find a quiet pub off the main road."

"Here's one, what about this?" shouted Reg.

"Too close for comfort," Eddie replied dismissively. "There's a better one at t'other side o' t'village."

Eddie drove on for another mile or so before pulling up alongside a small white-walled country inn. The sign above the door swinging slightly in the evening breeze announcing the venue as 'The Red Fox' The hard-standing for car parking was at the side of the pub and to some extent concealed the GPV from anyone driving up the main road.

"This looks all right to me, a cosy pub, buxom barmaids and a nice pint o'beer, you can't beat that". There was a distinct note of joyful anticipation in Eddie's voice at this unexpected prospect of a good night out.

It was a snug and cosy pub as they found out when they wandered in to the lounge bar. The low ceilings with the exposed beams and the big inglenook fireplace surrounded by gleaming brassware were an absolute revelation to Reg. He'd seen nothing like this before; his local pub only had a tap room and a best room, and the latter was too posh for him, even though it didn't have a carpet on the floor. This was magnificent, but people were looking at them now and he was feeling decidedly embarrassed. Eddie, however, walked boldly up to the bar, and Reg, trying his best to adopt the same military swagger followed him.

The barmaid, a middle-aged matronly type, greeted them with a cheerful smile, "Good evening, gentlemen."

"Good evening, my dear. Two pints of your very best bitter, please," Eddie requested, with all the man-of-the-world charm he'd developed in Blackpool. He leaned with one elbow resting nonchalantly on the bar and Reg sidled alongside and took up a similar position. The other customers had gone back to their conversations and Reg had a sly look around the place now that he was not the focus of attention. There were pictures on the walls, lovely flowered curtains at the windows and a carpet all over the floor, even under the tables.

"Here you are, sir. One and sixpence, please."

Eddie handed over half-a-crown and waited for the change.

"Thank you, sir, a shilling change."

The soldiers took their drinks to a table by the fireplace and sat down. "It's smashing is this, Eddie. I've never seen nowt like this before."

Eddie took a long steady drink from his glass and savoured the taste, "By, that tastes grand". He looked around as if noticing the room for the first time, "This is nowt special, son. Just stick around with me an' I'll show you some real pubs. Bloody sight better than the railway station, though, eh?"

Reg nodded enthusiastically, "Oh, aye, it is that".

"What annoys me," went on Eddie. "Is that we could a' been here all day. Bloody organisation up there". He broke off suddenly as he caught sight of two young women who had entered the room. "Look at the legs on that, will you?"

Reg whirled round in his chair.

"Not now, you dope!" he hissed. Reg blushed and turned back quickly, embarrassed by the tone of admonition in Eddie's voice. "You've got to do it discreet, Reg. Just watch me, you can't go blundering in like that. Women want you to be a bit sophisticated like."

The girls were obviously locals because they were chatting and laughing with the barmaid, and seemed very much at ease in the place. Eddie was watching them intently over Reg's shoulder; they were not unaware of his attention because when he winked at one of them she giggled coquettishly in a shrill voice and nudged her friend.

"Come on, Reg. Sup up, we're in here," Eddie urged.

Reg, taken by surprise, and faced with at least half a pint in his glass, struggled manfully to get it down whilst Eddie stood over him with his hand held out. Reg suddenly felt brimful of beer as he wiped his lips and chin with the sleeve of his jacket.

"Phew," he sighed, when he'd finished, the exercise almost beyond his swallowing capability. Fortunately, however, at that moment, an unexpected belch eased the pressure like an unblocked sink and the best bitter sank into his stomach like so much lead shot.

Whilst Reg was sorting out his internal problems Eddie had swaggered over to the bar in his best Erroll Flynn manner.

"Same again, sweetheart," he said to the barmaid in a tone of assumed familiarity, " ...and get one for yourself." He turned and smiled at the girls, "And what about you young ladies? Care to have a drink with two of His Majesty's fighting men?"

The girls giggled, but with a greater degree of coyness than embarrassment. "Don't mind if we do, do we, Marlene?" one of them said boldly.

"What'll you have then, sweetheart?" Eddie asked, very pleased with the way things were going.

"I'll have a port and lemon? What about you, Marlene?"

"Ooh, I'll have a gin and tonic, if you don't mind."

"Not at all ladies, a pleasure," Eddie said smoothly as he passed a ten shilling note over the bar. I must remember to get some money out of that dummy over there, he thought, before he falls off his bloody buffet.

"Come over here and join us," he said as he picked up the shorts and carried them over to the table. The girls followed obediently. "This is my friend, Reg, and I'm Eddie. Sit down and make yourself comfy, Marlene." He directed Marlene to a chair alongside his own and the other girl next to Reg. "What's your friend's name, then?"

"This is Barbara," she said giggling at her friend.

"Pleased to meet you both, then. Good health, and bottoms up, eh?" he added as an afterthought, a salacious leer on his face.

The girls shrieked. Reg laughed as well, he wasn't sure what at, but everybody seemed to be having a good time so he joined in.

That was the way the evening continued, he vaguely remembered giving his money to Eddie at one stage and somehow from then on the drinks just kept appearing in front of him. Each one presenting more of a challenge to get down than the previous one.

In an unexpected moment of lucidity he heard Marlene, was it Marlene? Well he heard one of them say, "What are you doing in these parts? We've never seen you around here before."

"Ah, shpecial mission, shweetheart," Eddie slurred, tapping the side of his nose conspiratorially. "Shtate shecret, can't tell you but, it's very important, I can tell you that!"

Reg forced himself to speak before he was engulfed in this fog again, funny that, he thought, the room was quite clear when they came in. "Eddie, shouldn't we be ..", another unexpected burp interrupted both his speech and his thoughts, "Exshcuse me", he paused, vacant eyed whilst he worked out what he wanted to say. "Eddie, shouldn't we, shouldn't we be getting back now?" Thank God, he'd managed to say it, and he sank back in his chair.

"Aye, in a minute or two, they'll not be needing us just yet," Eddie answered brightly. "Anyway, we're needed down here, aren't we girls?" He slipped his arm around Marlene's shoulder and gave her a squeeze.

"Ooh, you're a fast worker, you are", she laughed, but she didn't shake off his arm.

"I'm just making up for lost time, that's all. I should have met you years ago." For a minute Eddie had a cosy mental image of him and Marlene cuddling up together on a double seat in the back row of the Tennyson Picture Palace. Him and Erroll Flynn performing at the same venue, as it were. Eddie reached across and took hold of Marlene's hand;

she smiled up at him, obviously enjoying the attentions of one of his Majesty's fighting men almost as much as the gin and tonic.

Reg's desire to get back to his duty, seemed to have evaporated rapidly in the last ten minutes. Whilst his comrade-in-arms had been working his charms on the delectable Marlene, Reg had slumped back in his seat, oblivious to his surroundings. The sensory links between his brain and other faculties, tenuous at the best, had apparently suffered a total dislocation.

None of the four around the table noticed the faces of two men who peered through the window behind them. The men kept in the shadow of the wall, but it would have been immediately obvious to any observer, that they were only interested in two things; the army vehicle on the car-park and the two soldiers inside the hotel.

"Where would you like to go now girlsh?" asked Eddie, finishing off his pint with a flourish. "Fancy a drive in the moonlight, love?" He nudged Marlene suggestively.

"What do you think, Barbara? Shall we go for a drive?"

"If you like. Whatever you fancy."

"Here, I know what I'd fancy," quipped Eddie, amazed at his own wit. He just wished Reg was awake to appreciate it.

"We'll have none o' that, me lad," countered Marlene, giving him a playful push. "Well, not yet anyway". She giggled across at Barbara.

"Come on then, let'sh make a move," suggested Eddie. Even he had a little difficulty getting to his feet but his protective arm around Marlene's shoulders stabilised his movements from then on. The foursome took a rather noisy leave of the barmaid, with many a 'Good night and God Blesh' passing between them on their unsteady way to the door. Eddie, one arm around Marlene, was nuzzling her neck with his lips, the way his screen hero always did.

Barbara had her arm around Reg but more as a measure of support than as a prelude to romance. They stumbled out into the night and swayed round the corner towards their vehicle. Eddie fished the ignition keys out of his pocket with his free hand without disengaging himself from Marlene.

"You can ride in the front with me, shweetheart," he mumbled seductively in her ear. "Give ush a little kiss before we shtart." He pulled her towards him in an identical embrace to the one he'd seen Erroll use at the pictures last Saturday night. This was living.

"Excuse me miss, Military police"

What the hell was going on? Eddie felt his shoulders grabbed by a pair of strong hands as he was forcibly pulled away from Marlene.

"Yer, bloody what?", Eddie snarled as he turned aggressively towards the man behind him. That's all he did manage to say, however, because without the slightest hesitation, the man struck him a violent blow on the head with a short truncheon. With a grunt of pain and disbelief Eddie collapsed and lay inert over the side of the vehicle, his head over the back seat and his legs dangling over the back wheel.

"Sorry about this, miss," one of the men said with some authority. "But these men are dangerous deserters they are, we've been after them for days. It's back to prison for them now."

Reg was bundled, semi-comatose, into the back of the GPV alongside Eddie, and the men in dark raincoats raised their trilbies politely to the ladies, wished them goodnight, climbed into the front seats and drove away.

Even before the excited girls had finished telling their barmaid friend what had happened, the bodies of the two soldiers, stripped of their battle-dress tunics, were lying in a ditch at the side of the road. Each with a single bullet hole in the back of the head. O'Brady didn't mess about when it came to dealing with these bastards.

The Irishman and his German companion, now wearing British army jackets and caps, sped along the main road in the direction of Langham.

They were obviously very familiar with the area because they drove straight along the main street without hesitation, turned right under the bridges and up the bridleway towards Long Lane. The GPV bounced and bumped up the track as O'Brady kept up the speed. He slowed abruptly at the T-junction as the headlights picked up the shape of the 15cwt army truck.

"Damn it!", he snarled. His companion drew a long-barrelled pistol from his pocket. "Keep it hidden, Hans. They'll think we're on their side, don't fire unless you have to." O'Brady edged the GPV past the truck but there was no challenge; as far as O'Brady could see it appeared to be empty.

"We'll go up to the top of the lane and see what's happening. If there's nothing we can do we'll get out quickly." The Irishman looked at his companion for his approval.

"Ja, gut," responded the German. "Sehr schnell", he added with a nervous laugh.

"I wonder if the Scottish plan will still go ahead now?" O'Brady asked looking sideways at his companion.

The man shrugged, "Weiss nicht, Fragt Bergman. Wenn er ist nicht tod"

"You think they've got him? I told him it was too dangerous around here," O'Brady grumbled. "We should have concentrated on Scotland. Your chief in Germany happened to be of the same mind, if I remember correctly?"

The other man grunted some non-committal reply and clung tenaciously to the side panel as the GPV lurched and bucked its way up the lane. O'Brady glanced at his companion but did not pursue the topic and it soon left his mind altogether as the steering wheel twisted and turned in his grip as the track deteriorated the higher it got.

The lane ended at the top gate and they were then on the undulating grassy banks and limestone scars of the Langham Bottoms which Jack and Mike had walked across only a couple of hours before. The GPV shot down the slopes in frightening wheel-skidding slides, and then straight up the other side, wheels spinning desperately to maintain a grip, and the back-end swishing about like some metallic alligator trying to get onto a sandbank.

O'Brady and the German were elated at their progress; no ordinary vehicle could have survived this sort of treatment and they were both greatly impressed with the GPV's performance and were beginning to enjoy the exhilaration of this dashing drive across countryside.

The GPV hurtled up one rough track on a grassy mound and they found themselves overlooking the open moor; O'Brady braked hard and the vehicle skidded to a halt. Across a small valley immediately in front of them a battle was going on. The area was lit up by flashes of gunfire, and the crack of single shots were often drowned by the prolonged chattering of a machine gun. One group was in a depression in the moor and the other faction appeared to be in a superior position on the edge firing down at them.

O'Brady turned off the engine and he and his companion sat watching the action for some minutes whilst they considered their best line of approach.

Twenty

Ingleborough, Yorkshire Dales, 7th July 1939

Jack had left Mike on the rim of the plateau and he now moved in a crouching crawl across the darkening summit to take up a position with his four men on the far side of the shelter. They managed to get across remarkably easily as the Germans were completely absorbed in watching the approaching aircraft. Jack whispered brief instructions to his men and they waited nervously in the lee of the cairn for the moment to arrive. They heard the aeroplane's engines fire up some two hundred yards away, and peering round the stones shortly afterwards, Jack could see the wing flaps were down and the aircraft was coming in for another perfect landing.

The wheels hit the ground, the dust cloud came up and followed the plane as it rolled to a stop just short of the last of the landing lights. A spontaneous cheer went up from the waiting Germans and, as Jack watched, the door of the cabin opened and two men stepped out and hurried towards the waiting group.

"Now!", ordered Jack and he moved, pistol in hand towards the Germans. Two soldiers followed him and the other two went round the far side of the cairn. They quickly converged on the Germans who were still greeting the new arrivals.

"Stop there! Hands up!" Jack shouted.

There was a startled exclamation and the men whirled round.

"Stand still! Do not move!" Jack commanded.

The Germans, faced with four rifles and one pistol pointing directly at them from a distance of no more than five yards, made no aggressive movement and slowly raised their arms above their heads. Jack waved them into line and slipped behind them. Working quickly down the line he disarmed them while the soldiers covered them. He was just putting the last one in his haversack when two shots rang out in rapid succession. Jack whirled round and saw a flash of light in the cockpit of the aeroplane. The next moment there was a crescendo of noise as the pilot revved up the engines and the plane began taxi-ing around for take-off. Jack caught a fleeting glimpse of a figure on the ground before the whole scene was obscured by rising dust as the plane, its passenger door still flapping open, sped down the makeshift runway towards the edge of the summit.

As he watched in dismay there was a deafening report to his left followed immediately by a sharp cry of pain and the thud of a falling body. Jack whirled round, one of the Germans was lying face down on the ground.

"He went for his gun, sir," shouted one of the soldiers.

"Right, get them on the ground and search them again." Jack was utterly dejected, the plane was getting away; he considered firing at it but realised how futile that would be. It had reached the rim of the mountain and was beginning to lift off, it dropped slightly as it cleared the mountain. "Bloody hell", muttered Jack in disgust, "There it goes!"

As he spoke there was a brilliant flash of light and the whole rear part of the aeroplane disintegrated in a massive explosion. The scene was permanently etched on Jack's mind from that moment on. It seemed to happen in slow motion; first the brilliant flash of light, then the crashing blast of the explosion and then the flying burning debris showering the mountain side as the fireball of the main fuselage rolled down the mountainside into the valley below.

Everybody on the summit was stunned into immobility by this unexpected and dramatic conclusion to the flight. Jack was vaguely aware of someone calling his name. "Mike?" he shouted in reply, "Are you all right?" Mike was sitting on the ground holding his head, "Yeah, I think so, I think cracked my head on the aeroplane when I dived out." There was an abrasion

168

across his forehead but it didn't seem too serious, and Jack helped him to his feet.

"Did you get the others?" he enquired, as they walked across the summit. Jack explained what had happened and Mike expressed his satisfaction with the way things had gone.

"Well done, Jack. Let's get this lot down the mountain and see what's going on down there."

They left the dead body of the German where he'd fallen and Jack led the way off the summit, followed by Mike and the file of prisoners and army escort.

"What happened at the plane, then, Mike?" Jack asked when they were walking on the level stretch on the lower shoulder.

Mike snorted, "I nearly slipped up there, Jack. I waited until those chaps had got out, then I nipped over, opened the door, pointed my gun at the pilot and told him to get out. Unfortunately, there was a co-pilot in there as well, he fired over his shoulder straight at me. He must have had his gun in his hand when they landed. I dived out backwards and fired at the same time, then the engines revved up and it started moving. I just had time to pull the pin out and lob a grenade into the cabin before the back of the plane hit me and I was choked with dust."

"Quite a performance, eh?" Jack said, impressed with Mike's resourcefulness.

"Well, don't expect a repeat. We were very lucky, that's all. We didn't have enough manpower, we didn't have enough time, still we've put a stop to their little game, that's for sure."

As the group crested Little Ingleborough and commenced the final descent to the caves the darkness of the night was illuminated like a firework display by sustained flashes of gunfire around the Bar Pot area.

"Oh hell, look at that!" exclaimed Mike. "We'd better get a move on. Looks like trouble down there."

Leaving the soldiers to bring the prisoners down, Mike and Jack sped off down the hillside. However, long before they reached the level ground the heavy shooting had stopped; just the occasional flash briefly silhouetted the trees and crags at the edge of the crater.

They stopped by a large boulder and Mike shouted, "Bob!" And then again, when there was no reply, "Bob! Bob Bainbridge!"

Mike and Jack visibly relaxed when they heard a hoarse reply "Here sir, over here".

"Thank God for that," Mike whispered fervently, expressing Jack's feelings exactly, as they wriggled towards him.

They found the constable lying in a narrow cleft in a limestone crag directly overlooking the crater. His face was caked with dried blood and his right arm hung limply by his side.

"Are you all right, Bob?" Mike asked as he crawled up beside him.

"Not too bad, sir. I've been hit a couple o' times but nowt serious." Looking at him lying there, Jack thought Bob was understating the extent of his wounds; he didn't look too good at all. "I've got the buggers pinned down there now, " Bob said hoarsely. "They can't get out. We was attacked from behind, sir. Two of 'em came over the moor, they got the soldiers straight away, but I was over here and they didn't see me straight off." He nodded across the top of the crater, and Jack following his gaze could just make out some inert shapes on the far side. "One o' the Jerries got out of the hole and cleared off over that way with the other two." He waved vaguely in the direction of Long Lane with his uninjured arm. "I had to keep me head down when they opened up with the machine gun, that's when I got hit."

"You've done a great job, Bob.," Mike assured him. "We'll get you out of here as soon as we can. How many are still down there, do you think?"

"Two, possibly three."

"What about the girl, Bob?" Jack interjected. " Have you seen any sign of her at all?"

"No, I haven't lad. No sign at all."

"Right, you stay here, Bob. I'm not messing about any longer with this lot, if they don't come out now I'll blow 'em out. Come on, Jack".

The two men wriggled their way round the rim of the crater so they could look down into the depression towards the actual cave entrance. Mike shook his head sadly as they passed the sprawling lifeless bodies of the three British soldiers.

There had been no movement in the hollow since Mike and Jack had reached the constable. Mike cupped his hands and shouted through them, enunciating his words clearly, "You have two minutes to come out!". He paused a second and then added, "You are surrounded, come out now!". A shot rang out from below, Jack saw the flash and heard the whine of the bullet overhead as he and Mike flattened themselves to the ground.

"Right, that's it then," Mike said decisively. "You've asked for it". He unslung his haversack and took out a grenade and turned to Jack, "As soon as this goes off we'll both fire into the hole. I want to frighten them out, right?"

Jack checked his pistol, "Right!" he grunted.

Mike pulled out the pin and let the lever fly clear and dropped the grenade over the edge. They heard it clatter down the rocky slope and then it stopped, breathless silence. Three.. four... Jack counted. A tremendous explosion, amplified in the confined space of the hollow, seemed to rock the whole hillside. Instinctively Jack and Mike buried their heads in their arms as chunks of limestone and shrapnel whistled through the air. Mike was on his knees first and firing into the smoke-filled crater, after a second Jack did the same.

"Hold it, Jack", muttered Mike as a staggering figure emerged from the smoke, arms raised in the air.

"Kamerad, Kamerad, surrender!" the man shouted in between bouts of spluttering and coughing.

They waited until the man had stumbled his way up to ground level. Mike said, "Cover me", and slipped quickly round the rim, grabbed the man and pushed him to the ground face down.

"Where are the rest?" he demanded with his gun at the man's head.

"Dead, or wounded, can't walk", he gasped, still shaken by the explosion.

Mike waved Jack down to join him. The smoke had cleared now but the acrid smell caught in the back of the throat and made speech difficult.

Mike pulled the German to his feet, "You're going in first". He pushed the man in front of him and edged gingerly down the slope. Jack followed, gun at the ready, eyes flickering about from side to side. He need not have worried, it was as the man had said, the bodies of two men lay at the bottom of the crater path, probably victims of Bob's marksmanship from his position directly opposite. Mike gave them a cursory examination and the slow shake of his head told the others that they were past help.

"Any more?" Mike asked the prisoner.

The man shook his head.

"Any down there?" Mike pointed to the cave mouth.

"No, only the girl."

"Are you sure?", persisted Mike. "What about guards?"

The man shrugged, "No guards, no need. No way out."

Jack looked at the man's face, scratched, battered and bloody. He decided that the man was telling the truth. There was a hopeless look about him; he'd given up.

Bob's voice could be heard above them talking to the soldiers who had now arrived with their prisoners from the summit.

"I'd better just organise this lot and get Bob down to the village before we tackle the job of getting Ruth out of there," Mike said.

"I'll go down for her," Jack offered. "I'll just sort some gear out while you organise that lot. I hope there's enough rope to belay her up, that's all. It's a long climb out."

"Enough rope, Ja," the prisoner interrupted, eager to be helpful now that he'd accepted that everything was over.

Mike sent a man off at the double to bring the 15cwt truck to the top of Long Lane with instructions to fire a single shot when he got there, and to put on his headlights to guide the group to him. The prisoners were herded into the hollow and they sat there in a subdued little group under the watchful eyes of a soldier behind the Bren gun mounted at the top of the slope.

Mike wandered over to Bob Bainbridge when he was satisfied with the arrangements, "How's it going, old friend?" he asked sympathetically.

"Not so bad, sir," the constable retorted cheerfully. "I've been hit in this arm, but the bleeding seems to have stopped now."

"Right, let's have a look at it?" Mike gently tore away the shirt sleeve. There was a neat round hole in the upper arm and a line of caked blood down to the elbow. The lower sleeve was soggy with blood however and Mike was worried about how much blood Bob had lost. He was looking very pale in the face but that was difficult to assess properly in the moonlight. "It seems clean enough, Bob," he assured him. "Where else have you been hit?"

"My hand, same arm," he groaned painfully as he tried to lift it up.

"It's all right, keep it still," Mike said, as he examined it. It looked very bad, the hand had been shattered by a bullet and was an ugly raw mess with pieces of bone sticking out of the palm. Mike took a field dressing out of his bag and bound it up tightly. "That'll be all right until we get you to hospital, Bob. I'll just put a triangular bandage on to support the whole arm and then you're ready for off as soon as the truck gets here."

"Thanks, sir .. er, I'm sorry about those men over there, sir. We had them in the hole pinned down nicely when we was attacked from behind. I've no idea where they came from, they just started shooting when they were right on top o' us, them lads never had a chance."

"Look, Bob, you did everything you could, a first class job. You can't blame yourself for something like that."

Mike went down to the cave mouth and wriggled inside a short distance and called out "Ruth!" a number of times but the only sound that came back was the echo of his own voice and the sound of dripping water. It was unpleasantly dank and eerily dark; a very hostile environment he decided, as he made his way out into the balmy evening air. He was worried about Jack's intention to go down and search for Ruth immediately.

When Mike emerged from the cave mouth Jack was nearly ready to start. He had managed to equip himself with a carbide lamp, a helmet and a boiler suit from one of the Germans.

"Are you sure you'll be all right on your own, Jack?" Mike asked, a worried frown on his face. "Shouldn't we wait for a rescue party?"

"She's been down there too long already, Mike. I'll go and have a look now; if I can get her out, good, and if not...", he left the remainder unsaid. He didn't want to dwell on the possibilities, he wanted to get moving, to get on with the job now.

"All right, but take care, and good luck. I'll wait here until you get back."

Twenty One

Gaping Gill, Yorkshire Dales, 7th July 1939

Jack's initial bravado and enthusiasm for the underground rescue dissipated rapidly when he actually got inside the cave entrance. On previous descents he'd had the support and camaraderie of his caving friends and it had been a cheerful enjoyable affair. Now it was quiet, hostile and lonely; he felt very isolated and was only too well aware that help, if needed, would be very difficult to find. What if he couldn't find Ruth straight away, and his carbide ran out? Suppose Ruth didn't have the strength to get back up the rope ladder? Desperately trying to exclude these and other negative thoughts from his mind he made his way to the top of the big pitch. He found it surprisingly easy as the route was clearly marked and either fixed-ropes, or ladders, helped him down the difficult sections.

Jack uncoiled the heavy hemp rope ladder and lowered it down the big pitch. He checked the belay for the ladder and it seemed firm enough. He was glad to see that there was also a large coil of climbing rope tied-off to a projecting rock. I'll need that to get Ruth up, he thought; the only trouble is, I'll have to come up first without a top rope.

Jack shouted down the dark shaft a couple of times and listened carefully but he could hear nothing but the echoing of his own voice and the constant dripping and splashing of falling water.

Here goes, he said to himself, as he struggled over the edge. It was always difficult getting a good grip on the rungs where the ladder was tight against the rock, and it was with some relief that his hands were able to find a rung. Once started, and comfortable on the ladder, Jack developed a regular movement of feet and arms and descended quite quickly. He was particularly careful to keep the flame of his carbide lamp away from the rope sides of the ladder. Having once smelled burning hemp when on a ladder a hundred feet above the ground, Jack had a caution instilled into him which was more akin to a phobia than to a simple worry.

Jack moved away from the bottom of the pitch and headed along the passage, pistol in hand, towards the main chamber of Gaping Gill. He was heading for a side passage which led to a dry chamber called Sand Cavern. He knew that this was a likely place for the Germans to use as a base as he remembered some of his fanatical caving friends once camping there during their summer holidays. When he'd asked why they hadn't gone to Morecambe like everyone else one of them had retorted, "Well, for a start there's more bloody sand down here, and it's a damn sight warmer!"

He soon reached this narrower passage which branched off left from the main one and, moving very cautiously now, edged his way up towards the dry chamber. He was wise to do so because after a dozen or so yards he caught the glimmer of light ahead. Heart beating rapidly and pistol gripped firmly in his hand Jack crept forward, placing his feet on the rocky ground with infinite care. As the passage widened he crouched down and slowly advanced until he could see into a well-lit sizeable chamber. There was no one in sight but all the impedimenta of an underground camp were there. The tilly lamp on the table in the centre of the cave threw a pale yellow light over the row of camp beds and was reflected in the cooking pans on the large portable camping stove. Jack breathed more easily now that he realised the place was deserted and he moved across to the kitchen area, half expecting to find a pan of warm stew on the stove, but everything was immaculately clean and the tea pot was stone cold.

Jack left the relative hospitality of Sand Cavern and retraced his steps to the main passage. He turned left and hurried along to the main chamber; this was a lot less impressive than it had been in the daylight. His headlamp picked up the falling spray of the stream, diffused into a thousand droplets by its long fall from the surface. The boundaries of the chamber seemed limitless and the range of his lamp was not sufficient to reach to the walls. Jack shouted out Ruth's name but his words seemed to be absorbed into the general noise of splashing water, echoing sound and the all-pervading blackness around him.

Where the hell can she be? He thought, panic momentarily taking hold of him. She's in here somewhere, she'll be hiding, she'll be keeping out of the way.

Taking heart from this cooler approach to the problem Jack moved round the perimeter of the chamber in an anti-clockwise direction. There were various possible exits out of the main chamber as well as many blind passages at different levels. Jack kept the chamber wall in view on his right hand side; every twenty paces he stopped, cupped his hands round his mouth and bellowed out her name.

He'd got about a third of the way round the chamber in this halting fashion when the sound of falling rocks above and to his right caused him to duck down and cover his head with his arms. "Bloody hell!" he exclaimed involuntarily from his crouching position, then realising the implication, he shouted at the top of his voice, "Ruth, is that you? It's Jack, Jack Warrendale!"

Jack's heart leapt at the answer, "Jack? Is it you?", there was a tremulous note of disbelief in Ruth's voice. She was sitting in a cave entrance some fifteen feet up some loose scree against the chamber wall.

"Here, Ruth", Jack shouted unable, to conceal his delight. "Can you get down all right?" There was no answer but he didn't need one because his headlamp picked up the slight figure scrambling and sliding down the scree: the next minute she was in his arms.

"Oh, Jack", she sobbed. "Thank God it's you."

Jack was glad it was her too; she felt very snug in his arms with her face in the side of his neck. "Are you all right?" he said after a minute or two. " We've been worried sick about you".

She moved back slightly and the smile which crossed her dirt-encrusted face, warmed up the whole underground chamber for Jack. "I'm a thousand times better than I was five minutes ago," she laughed.

He put his arm around her shoulders, "Let's get out of here. You've had a hard time." They moved very slowly and Jack told her briefly what had happened since they'd last met at the station. Ruth was amazed to hear how many people were involved and how much had been done.

When he'd finished she murmured, "Thanks to you, Jack," and when her arm squeezed his waist Jack forgot about his damp bedraggled state, the fatigue, and his freezing feet, and just felt suffused by a warmth of feeling and well-being. The only thing that dimmed Jack's star was the fact that Ruth had neither seen nor heard anything of his uncle.

They made a brief visit to Sand Cavern and Jack recharged Ruth's headlamp before making their way to the foot of the ladder.

Jack wrapped the end of the rope around Ruth's waist, tied a bowline in it and pulled it tight. He showed her how to climb the ladder and told her to take her time; she would be quite safe as he would have the lifeline on her from above. He didn't tell her about the dangers of his climbing the ladder without a top rope, but he didn't want to dwell on that either.

"When I get up," Jack explained. "I'll tighten the rope, so when you feel it's taut you shout 'that's me!' then when I say 'start climbing!' you come up. Remember keep your arms opposite your face, don't reach up, and mind the flame of your lamp on the rope". He smiled at her and they kissed gently on the lips, "see you in a minute then."

Jack was so buoyant that he felt like running up the ladder, but he contained his exuberance and plodded steadily upwards, pausing occasionally to rest his arms. He knew it was a long haul and the important thing was to get up safely. When he glanced down between his feet he could see the tiny point of light from Ruth's helmet, what a comfort that was. Looking up, however, the ladder disappeared into the gloom above, a seemingly endless series of rungs. The rhythm of lifting feet and moving hands occupied his mind for the rest of the climb but he was very relieved to feel the ladder tight against the rock where it went over the edge of the pitch. Very carefully he positioned himself so that he could reach above the edge and get a firm grip on the side of the ladder and heave himself up on to the ledge.

He recovered his breath and flexed and relaxed his arms a few times before pulling in the life-line. He heard Ruth shout when the rope got tight and he tied off the slack behind him to a flake of rock, slipped the line over his shoulder and shouted to her to start climbing. The strong protective feeling he had towards her was heightened during the climb. He knew how worried she felt and he could feel the contact with her body through the rope. He could tell when she faltered, when she rested, even when she was finding climbing difficult as the ladder twisted. She was having to rest more frequently now and Jack could feel more of her bodyweight on the rope.

He stood overlooking the chasm and shouted down words of encouragement, "You're nearly there now, Ruth. I've got you safe on the top rope, just take it steady; stop when you want to".

Very slowly Ruth's headlight got nearer the top and he could hear her laboured breathing long before she reached the topmost rungs. Jack's arms and shoulders were aching but he kept the rope tight and, as Ruth's helmet and lamp came level with the ledge, he reached over and unceremoniously grabbed her by the back of the boiler suit and pulled her over the edge as though landing a large fish.

They collapsed in each other's arms. Ruth was exhausted, breathless and trembling after the ordeal. She lay there gasping and for a minute or two was unable to speak. Jack muttered words of comfort into her ear as he held her close, and to his surprise even words of endearment seemed to come naturally to his lips.

After a few minutes she recovered sufficiently to move up to the shorter final ladder.

"Soon be out now, love," he said cheerfully. "This is nothing compared to the last one."

Ruth half-smiled, "Just get me out, Jack. I've had enough of this".

There were no further problems and when they reached the top of that ladder they could smell the warm fresh air from the surface.

"Oh, Jack, just smell that glorious fresh air," Ruth said with excitement in her voice. "I can't wait to get out of here. I'll tell you something Jack Warrendale, I'm never going down one of these again."

Jack smiled, "Nor me." He took Ruth's arm and led her out of the cave mouth and into the crater outside. They stood together hand in hand and breathed in the sweet moorland air.

"Hello there", It was Mike calling down from the top of the track. "Am I glad to see you, both of you."

Arm in arm Jack and Ruth climbed up the track out of the crater. "Ruth, allow me to introduce Inspector Mike Bannerman," and turning to Mike, "Mike, this is Ruth Lancaster, as you'll have guessed."

"Delighted to meet you at last." said Mike holding out his hand with smile. "Are you all right? You've had a tough time of it, I'm afraid."

"I'm fine, thanks," she answered brightly, "In fact, I've never felt so fine in all my life, " she said, with a shy glance at Jack.

"How's Bob, Mike?" Jack enquired.

"Fortunately, not as bad as we first thought. He can walk all right so I've sent him down in the truck with the prisoners and escort, they're going straight on to Settle."

The bodies of the dead, English and German, had been brought to the side of the track and were lying undifferentiated side by side covered by khaki groundsheets.

Ruth looked at them silently, as Mike explained gravely, "We lost three men here today. They had more men than we thought, it was a very well-organised spy cell."

"Where's Bergman?" Ruth asked. "Is he one of these?"

"'Fraid not," said Mike. "According to Bob Bainbridge he got away down the track when the German reinforcements arrived."

"Where the hell did they come from? That's what I'd like to know," Jack queried. "I thought we'd accounted for all the groups in the area, didn't you, Mike?"

"Yes, I must admit, I did. It's something we're going to have to look into when we get down." He looked contemplatively into the gloomy shakehole for a minute, "Well, that's about all we can do up here today, Jack, I'm afraid there'll be a fair bit of unpleasant tidying up to do tomorrow, both here, and on the summit.

Jack nodded, remembering the crumpled body lying on the summit and the remains of the aeroplane and crew scattered somewhere in the depths of Black Shiver.

"Let's get Ruth down to civilisation," Mike suggested, breaking into Jack's thoughts.

"Ruth can get a hot bath at the farm," said Jack. "I'm sure Aunt Dorcas will be grateful for some female company."

"Ooh, that sounds absolutely heavenly," Ruth agreed enthusiastically. "I can't wait to get cleaned up. Do you now how long I've been like this?"

"As a matter of fact, we do," answered Mike. "I followed you up here twenty four hours ago, .though to tell the truth, it seems more like twenty four weeks ago."

Jack put a protective arm around Ruth as they followed Mike down to the farm. A single lamp burned in the porch and afforded a welcome beacon as they reached the last pasture. The house was quiet as Aunt Dorcas had retired to bed some three hours before, but Gemmy's initial bark, the stoking-up of the fire and the rattle of pans soon aroused her and she was down and fussing over them in a matter of minutes.

Their dirty, dishevelled appearance had shocked the old lady at first, but her fears were allayed by their good spirits, and she busied herself preparing the large tin bath by the fire and organising some pots of tea.

"Eeeh, ye look like three chimley sweeps," she remarked. "You can't be going to t'village like that," she added, when Jack told her that they had to go down there. "You get yersen weshed and have a pot o' tea, then you can go".

The old lady's common-sense convinced them and Jack and Mike had a quick wash and brush-up and then sat at the table with hot steaming mugs of tea clasped in their hands.

"Is there anything I can do to help?" Ruth offered.

"Yes, there is," Jack said affectionately. "Get something to eat, have a hot bath by the fire and look after yourself."

"I agree," said Mike. "We'll not be long, I hope, but we have to see what's happened down the valley. We're going to need your help and advice tomorrow."

Ruth smiled sweetly, "Thanks very much, you're very kind. You will take care, won't you?"

Jack's heart missed a beat, he was sure the latter remark had been intended for him. Surprisingly, the fatigue he had felt earlier seemed to have disappeared, and he felt quite sprightly as he and Mike set off down to the village in the moonlight.

Twenty Two

Langham, Yorkshire Dales, 7th July 1939

Langham slept peacefully in the pale unearthly light as Jack and Mike walked down the main street. It would have taken a particularly observant eye to notice the twitch of the curtain at number 45 as Mrs Thornton, note book on knee, noted down yet another pair of smugglers passing through. It had been one of the busiest nights she'd ever experienced; army wagons, a square boat-like thing, a big black motor car; she had a list of them all and she intended to call on Constable Bainbridge first thing in the morning with all the details.

The Old Crown was in darkness apart from the light in the night porter's little office.

"Let's check out this place whilst we're passing, Jack. I don't think that even Bergman would have the cheek, or be stupid enough, to come back here though."

The night porter was asleep at his desk, head resting on his arms on an open copy of the Daily Mirror. He shot upright violently, eyes staring wildly when Mike rapped on the desk with the butt of his pistol. "Www...Wwhat's up?" he stammered, fear coming into his eyes when he saw the gun.

"Police", Mike said abruptly. "Mr Bergman. Is he here?"

The porter shook his head, "N-N-No, sir." He stuttered. "He left about two hours ago. Took his bags and everything."

"How did he go?...Taxi?"

"No sir, his own motor car."

Mike, and Jack looked at each other in surprise. This was news to them.

"Own car?" Mike queried. "Which was that?"

"He had a motor car in the garage round the back, sir. A black one, a Mercedes Benz I think it was, sir."

Mike looked at Jack in dismay, "Bloody hell," he cursed. "We missed that."

Turning back to the porter he said brusquely, "Right man, listen. I want Bergman's room sealed up until I come tomorrow. No cleaners in, nobody. And the same with the garage, nobody to go in at all. Have you got that?"

"Yes sir, I'll tell the manager. He comes on at nine in the morning. Who shall I tell him called?"

"Inspector Bannerman, Scotland Yard".

The man's jaw dropped and his eyes widened; Jack moved behind Mike's back to suppress a smile at the man's ludicrous expression.

"Let's just have a look round the garage," Mike suggested as they came out of the hotel. "You never know, if they went in such a rush they might have left some clues behind?"

It was dark on the car park behind the building. Jack could see the outline of a row of wooden garages and they made their way towards them. The door of one was unlocked and Mike unfastened the hasp. "This'll be the one Bergman used, I'll ... ", he broke off abruptly. "Oh no ..."

Jack looked over Mike's shoulder. Even in the darkness of the garage he could still make out the distinctive shape of the GPV, "Now we know how Bergman got away, don't we?", he muttered. "Somebody came up Long Lane and over the moor in this, took Bob and his group by surprise, and whisked Bergman away."

Mike sighed, "I'm afraid you might be right, Jack. That is annoying. How the hell did they get hold of this, though?" Mike had gone further into the garage and was feeling his way down the side of the vehicle when Jack heard Mike's sudden intake of breath.

"What's up?" he queried urgently.

"Definitely something wrong here, look at this!" He stepped out of the garage and held up his hands. "Blood, and lots of it, all over the back seat."

"The soldiers? Or one of them wounded?"

"I fear it might be one of ours, " Mike said quietly. "Let's get down to the station and find out. We'll have to walk, they haven't left the keys as far as I can see."

As they turned the corner into the station forecourt they were heartened to see the lights from the waiting room and stationmaster's office, and hear the voices of the men inside.

They were met by the stationmaster himself, in full uniform, when they entered the office. Sergeant Mann was sitting at the desk, and he rose to his feet when he saw Mike. "No trouble on Ewes Cross, sir", he said immediately. "There were two of 'em. They were just standing there with their mouths wide open as though they were shell-shocked after you'd blown the aeroplane up, we just walked up and caught 'em. They're in the waiting room drinking tea with my men at the moment. How did you go on, sir?"

Mike went over the main details briefly; the stationmaster and the sergeant listened in silence and with rapt attention until he'd finished.

"Cor," the sergeant said. "You've 'ad it a bit rough, sir. By the way sir, Mr Winterburn 'ere, 'as 'eard from the Beck Fell group and they're all right as well." He glanced down at a note on the desk, "They've taken two prisoners and there's one dead Jerry. I telephoned Settle and they're sending a Black Maria up. I 'ope I did right, sir?"

"Excellent, Sergeant. I'm proud of you, and you too, Mr.Winterburn. You've both done a first class job." The stationmaster seemed to visibly expand with pride, and Jack, standing by the doorway feared the buttons on his jacket might not be able to stand the strain. He had a fleeting vision of the buttons flying off in all directions and spattering against the opposite wall. He smiled to himself at the thought of Harold standing there, chest expanded, in his regulation railway vest.

"By the way, the two soldiers we left here in reserve?" Mike asked after a moment.

"On patrol, sir", Winterburn answered smartly. "They left me to look after the telephone, sir. I've logged all the calls on that paper on the desk." Mann pushed the paper across the desk to Mike. Jack could see that the only in-coming call was the one from Constable Birkwith over in Beckley.

"They said they'd be back in an hour, sir, but that was about three hours ago...", Winterburn's voice tailed off indecisively.

"Percival must have called them out to help him," Mike said thoughtfully. "Did you see anything of them up your way, Sergeant?"

"Not a thing, sir."

Mike thought for a minute and then told Mann and Winterburn about the finding of the bloodstained GPV in the hotel garage. The information was received in silence as the implication dawned on them. Mike continued, "Right, Beck Fell is clear, so is Ewes Cross so this side is finished, that only leaves Percival's group in doubt. Jack, we'd better take the car and a couple of men and go and find him. The full moon's coming up and I'd rather get things sorted out now than later."

Jack nodded.

"Sergeant, I want you to stay here and see to the evacuation of the prisoners, if you will please?"

"Very good, sir!"

"But be on your guard, Bergman might have gone or he might not. There are at least three of them on the loose and we've lost enough men already."

"Right, sir. I'll 'ave two men on guard all the time from now on."

Mike drove his car slowly up the hill towards Kingsdale, Jack was in the passenger seat next to him and two policemen were in the back seat, rifles across their knees. Mike had to change down to first gear at one point as the weight of the occupants nearly proved too much for the pulling power of the engine.

They had just reached the crest of the hill, and a distinct note of relief had entered the engine tone, when a figure in a British army uniform leapt out in front of them. The beam of the headlights picked out the rifle and glinted on the fixed bayonet pointing at the windscreen; Mike slammed on the brakes. The policemen in the back cursed at the sudden jolt, as they and their accoutrements crashed against the front seat. When Mike wound down his window they heard the guard calling out in a tremulous voice, "Halt! Er.. who goes there? Friend or foe?"

"Oh, bloody hell," groaned Mike. "It's Fred Karno himself. You'd better get out Jack and tell him we're friends before he bayonets the bloody bonnet."

"Perkins, sir," the man replied to Mike's question. The group were in the shelter of the wall where Percival had made his base. Perkins was overjoyed at the arrival of the authorities, some peculiar things had happened up on that hillside tonight and he hadn't known what to do for the best. Mr Percival had gone after that man on the moor and left him here on his own to guard the road, then there'd been those shots up there, and after that, a massive explosion, and over on the big mountain there'd been more explosions and a blazing ball of fire.

"Did anyone come up or down this road this evening?" Mike asked after he'd listened to this tale from Perkins.

"No, sir. You were the first."

"When you heard the shots did you go up to see what was going on?" Mike continued.

"No, sir. My orders was to stay 'ere and guard the road, sir."

"We'd better go up there and find out where Mr. Percival's got to then. Jack will you come with me? Constable Dent and Private Perkins, you'd better come as well."

"What about the road, sir? I'm supposed to guard the road," Perkins objected petulantly, reluctant to leave its relative safety for the unknown dangers of the heights.

"PC Garsdale will control the road, it's more of a police duty anyway. I need you with us as you heard where the shots came from."

Perkins looked far from happy about this, he seemed to have become rather attached to his guard post at the roadside. However, he followed Jack and the rest of the group up through the crags and on to the Turbary Road; more or less the exact route that Percival and Thomas had followed on their ill-fated trip earlier that evening.

They walked silently in single file along the track, the moonlight cast their shadows which rippled eerily alongside them on the grass. What a beautiful scene, Jack thought. In his present state of mind, of course, everything had acquired an extra glow, but Kingsdale by moonlight had introduced another dimension altogether. He must bring Ruth up here sometime, she would love it. Cocooned in the comfort of these and similar romantic thoughts, Jack was almost on top of the inert body of Second Lieutenant Percival before he saw it. He stopped abruptly and raised his hand; the others stopped in their tracks behind him.

"Oh, God", muttered Mike when he came up to Jack. "Poor young bugger never had a chance by the look of it." Percival lay there flat on his back, a look of injured surprise on his pale young face and sightless blue eyes staring vacantly at the stars. The bullets had ripped through his Sam

188

Browne and into his chest and a mass of congealed blood stained the front of his tunic.

"Perkins!" Mike ordered, "Groundsheet! Cover Mr. Percival up please." Mike knelt down and tried to prise the revolver out of Percival's hand, but death's grip was not so easily released. Mike did not persist as the action seemed somehow to be lacking in dignity, and so the Brigadier's birthday present remained clutched in his nephew's hand for the rest of that night.

"Let's move on a bit, Jack." Mike suggested. "I'll bet the other chap's around here somewhere," he muttered quietly.

This part of the fellside was enclosed by a series of stone walls which swept down from the upper slopes of Gragareth on their left and crossed the Turbary Road every three or four hundred yards or so.

Jack passed through the next gate which was only a matter of yards from Percival's fallen body, and obviously the place from which the ambush had occurred. By the light from Dent's police lamp, a cluster of spent cartridge cases at the other side of the gate confirmed the theory. Mike picked one up, "9mm, probably a Luger", he said tersely.

They headed along the track in single file towards the next wall.

"What's that, sir? I heard something," the constable behind Jack whispered urgently. Jack stopped and looked at the young policeman who stood with his head held to one side in an exaggerated listening posture.

The others raised their heads and adopted similar postures. For a moment they looked like a group of bronze figures in a sculpture-park. Suddenly the classical formation disintegrated as each member of the group ducked simultaneously as though choreographed by some invisible director. "It's someone shouting," muttered Mike. "Spread out, and keep your heads down!"

He moved forward in a crouching gait and, after a moment's hesitation, the others followed. Half way between the walls they heard the shout again, this time the word "Help" was very clear. Twenty yards from the next gate Mike stopped, a dark shape was crouching by the gate, man or sheep? He couldn't be sure in this light. The rest of the group joined him and trained their guns on the object of suspicion.

"Who's there?" Mike shouted.

The others ducked, fully anticipating a volley of shots from some carefully prepared ambush.

Jack was more surprised by what actually happened, than he would have been at fusilade of shots. A calm voice replied, "Joshua Warrendale, farmer, High Top Farm, Langham."

"W-W-What? Uncle Joss!" shouted Jack in disbelief.

"Keep down, Jack, for God's sake!" Mike ordered,. "I don't trust these bastards at all, it might be a trap."

"What are you doing there?" Mike bellowed towards the gate.

"I've been held prisoner for the past week," came the reply. "an' I've been chained to this bloody gate half the night," he added grumpily.

"It's my uncle's voice all right," Jack confirmed.

"Ask him if he's on his own, Jack. Tell him who you are," Mike whispered.

"Uncle Joss, this is your nephew!"

"Jack?" his uncle questioned, a note of bewilderment in his voice. "Jack? What the hell are you doing up here?"

"Listen, Uncle. Are you alone?" Jack continued.

"Aye, they went down the valley hours ago, two on 'em."

Even after this assurance their final approach was made with very great circumspection, the picture of the body lying by the other gate was still fresh in their minds.

The reunion, when it came, between uncle and nephew was a joyful affair, they embraced, shook hands and hugged each other with relief. Whilst Perkins and Dent worked on his release from the gate, Joss explained how he'd been abducted and where he'd been kept all the time. He told them how his captors had handcuffed him to the gate and then blown up the equipment in the cave when they realised that their operation had been discovered.

Mike was particularly interested in the Irishman that Joss mentioned and asked for a description.

"Ah", he said, thoughtfully. "That explains a few things, at least. That sounds very much like O'Brady. He's a ruthless one, and he'd welcome the chance to kill a British soldier, or anybody else who got in his way, for that matter. So, the IRA is involved in this too? We thought the Germans might be giving them help over in Ireland, but it looks as though they're operating over here as well now."

When Joss was free and had got the circulation back in his chafed wrist they retraced their steps along the track. They passed Percival's body in silent respect. Mike told them he would arrange for a party to come here first thing in the morning to remove the body and search for the other missing soldier. Joss pointed out where he thought his captors had gone down the valley. He'd seen the beam of a flashlight as they went over the hill in the direction of Westinghall. That would explain why Thomas had not seen them on the road; lucky man, thought Mike, if he had seen them he wouldn't be alive now.

Harold Winterburn at the railway station was overjoyed to see Joss. What a night this had been. And he, Stationmaster Winterburn, one of the central figures. His office, the main operational headquarters. What a story he had to tell in the village.

Mike spent the next three quarters of an hour on the telephone. He rang Settle to check on the condition of Bob Bainbridge; satisfactory, but they were keeping him in overnight for observation. He gave an interim report to the duty officer at Special Branch in London, and then contacted Leeds

Police to enquire about the position regarding Ruth's family. Apparently they had been visited by a couple of thugs shortly before the police arrived. Three armed plainclothes officers waited for their return and when they walked in an hour later they were arrested without any trouble. Finally Mike telephoned Jim Birkwith in Beckley to congratulate him on his successful work at Beck Fell Farm. The police van had already taken away the prisoners, Jim told him, and he had already sorted out some temporary accommodation for the other policemen.

"Well, that's it, Jack," said Mike with a long drawn out sigh. "That's all we can do tonight. I suggest we get your uncle back home and get some sleep. We've a lot of tidying up to organise tomorrow, three missing men to find and Bergman and his two cronies to look for, although I reckon they'll be well away now. Where is your uncle, by the way?"

"Drinking tea in the waiting room with Harold and Sergeant Mann, I think," laughed Jack.

"Right, let's go. Mann and his merry men will have to bunk down here for the night. We'll need them tomorrow."

What a joyful and emotional night it was at High Top Farm. Aunt Dorcas wept tears of joy at Joss's safe return and the dog almost whirled itself into insensibility. Ruth sat by the fire with her wet hair wrapped turban-style in a towel and looked fresh-faced, very young and eminently beautiful in one of his aunt's dressing gowns, at least that's what Jack thought.

Ruth was moved by the elderly couple's reunion and even more so when Mike told her that her own parents were quite safe and well. Ruth explained that Bergman had threatened to harm them if she did not co-operate with him. She also told them that she had been sent up to Langham in response to PC Bainbridge's report about suspicious strangers in the area. Apparently the Home Office had received many such reports, and agents had been despatched to various coastal areas in the north-east, and airfields in Kent and East Anglia to check them out. She'd been studying a picture of Bergman shortly before Jack's arrival in the carriage and when Jack had gone for the tea she'd slipped out to the toilet and come face to face with Bergman in the corridor. Unfortunately he'd noticed that immediate shock of recognition, or had already spotted her studying his picture, and he and a another man had bundled her off the train at Peterborough at gun-point. Luckily for her, in the rush, one of them had grabbed Jack's suitcase from the rack above her seat. She looked across at Jack and smiled sweetly at him, "and what a marvellous job you did from thereon, Jack." Jack nearly dissolved with ecstasy, felt himself blushing, mumbled something about it being nothing and stood up.

"It looks as though these two will be chatting all night," he said, nodding at his Aunt and Uncle.

"Less o' yer cheek, yer young monkey," his aunt remarked good humouredly. "We'll go to bed when we're ready. By the way, I've put Ruth in your room, so you'll have to sleep on that camp bed in Mike's room."

"Yea, that's fine, thanks Aunty."

Mike and Ruth had also risen to their feet and after wishing Dorcas and Joss goodnight they trooped upstairs. On the landing outside Jack's old room Ruth turned and lightly kissed Jack on the cheek, "See you in the morning, gentlemen," she said as she slipped through the doorway.

Needless to say all the occupants of High Top Farm slept soundly for what remained of that night. It had been an exhausting and very momentous day, to try and think about all that had happened was impossible, sleep overtook them all before they'd even started. Jack slept soundly too, a blissful smile on his lips and a hand held gently to his cheek.

Twenty Three

Langham, Yorkshire Dales, 8th July 1939

Next morning, Mike took Ruth and Jack down to the village in the car. They stopped at Bob Bainbridge's cottage to have a word with his wife and were pleasantly surprised to find that Bob was already back from hospital. His rubicund features lit up in a broad smile when he saw them and it was obvious that his wounds didn't bother him unduly. He expressed his pleasure at meeting Ruth and was even more delighted when Jack told him about his uncle's safe return. Bob insisted on going down to the railway station with them, he could help tidy up some of the loose ends he told them.

Mike turned the Rover into the station forecourt and braked suddenly and uttered an exclamation of surprise, "What the hell? What's all this?"

The others made no immediate comment but just sat there staring at the scene before them. Drawn up in a neat row in front of the station was a collection of military and police vehicles; there were two large trucks crammed with soldiers, a signals van, two khaki staff cars with pennants drooping, two police cars, a large black Bentley limousine, and an assortment of army despatch riders and military police motorcyclists. It was as if they had driven into the middle of a military and police transport revue.

"The Langham Motor Show?" Jack suggested .

At the entrance to the station they could see the uniformed figure of the Stationmaster, strutting along, official folder tucked under his arm, as though reviewing the display and preparing to judge the entrants.

"Great to see the cavalry's arrived at last," muttered Mike.

"And all the top brass they could find, by the look of it, sir," added Bob.

"That other big truck will be carrying all the forms to be filled in," Ruth said dryly.

They all laughed and Mike remarked, "You obviously work for the same sort of people as me, Ruth."

He parked his car round the back next to the 15cwt truck and they walked in a group towards the office. They were met on the steps by an army officer dressed in khaki tunic, fawn breeches and highly polished riding boots. He wore the crown of a major on his shoulder and twitched his swagger stick against the side of his boot impatiently.

"Major Bulshaw, Adjutant, 1st battalion West Yorkshire Regiment," he said briskly.

Mike introduced himself and his three companions. The major shook hands with Mike and nodded curtly to the others.

"The Brigadier is waiting to see to see you now, sir. The Assistant Chief Constable is with him," he added.

Mike raised his eyebrows in surprise, and he and Bob exchanged glances. "Oh," he murmured. "Is he now?"

"They've been waiting for some time, sir", interjected Bulshaw. "Would you follow me, please?"

Since it was fairly obvious that the invitation did not extend to the others Mike turned to them and said, "I'll see you all later, you'll probably get a pot of tea in the office."

Mike followed the adjutant along the platform towards the waiting room. Jack chuckled quietly at the contrast between the officer's immaculate turn-out and Mike's dirt-stained clothing and scuffed boots.

Bob noticed Jack's amusement and commented quietly, "We need more of the latter, and less of the former in this sort of game, if you ask me?"

Jack was inclined to agree.

Ruth used the time to telephone her chief at the Home Office and make a verbal report. She was a bit nervous about doing this and confided her feelings to Jack. "I'll have a fair bit of explaining to do," she sighed.

"I shouldn't let it worry you, Ruth," Jack said confidently. "If it hadn't been for you we wouldn't have got on to them at all. You spotting Bergman started the whole thing. Look, if you can beat the Germans you can deal with the bureaucrats, surely?"

Ruth smiled and squeezed his hand affectionately, "Yes, of course I can, thanks, Jack." Jack went out on to the car park and wandered amongst the vehicles whilst she made the telephone call. If only they'd had this lot here twenty four hours earlier, he thought, what a difference that would have made.

It was over an hour before Mike rejoined them, and his face showed signs of strain and fatigue. "Well, it's out of our hands now. You know, that was worse than the top of Ingleborough." he muttered wryly. "I just hope I made the right decisions. They put all sorts of doubt in your mind."

"You did the best you could, sir", Bob said stoutly. "Nobody could have done more than you."

"I agree," supported Jack. "You couldn't have tackled the job in any other way".

Mike smiled his appreciation, "Thanks for your support, both of you. I couldn't have managed without you, I know that". He turned to Ruth, "This is a terrific team we've got here."

She smiled, "You don't have to tell me; look what you did for me. Saved my life, rescued me from the labyrinth and caught the villains."

Jack felt the warmth in his cheeks when her eyes rested on his. Fortunately, the crunch of wheels on gravel outside distracted them and drew their attention to the window. The army lorries were moving out with their motor cycle escorts and the convoy headed up the lane towards the main road.

"They're going up to recover the bodies," Mike said sadly. "We lost a lot of men, I'm afraid. Three at the pothole, one and possibly two on Gragareth, and two more are still missing." He sighed, obviously still very conscious of his responsibilities. They turned again to the window as the Bentley and staff cars started up and moved away, "They're staying at the Falcon Hotel in Settle, that's going to be the Command HQ," Mike informed them.

"Bit like the Great War, wouldn't you say, sir?" Bob remarked acidly. "Not too near the front line, and rather more comfortable."

They all laughed and Mike said, "Come on, I'll buy you all a drink in The Flying Dutchman. Oh, and that reminds me, talking of flying Dutchmen, I forgot to tell you that a black Mercedes Benz was seen near the docks in Heysham in the early hours of this morning. They put out a general alert to all west coast ports last night after I'd telephoned in. Apparently one of the customs men had seen the car earlier; there was no sign of Bergman or the other two, though. They've either skipped the country, or that's what they want us to think. It might just be a blind and they could be enjoying the hospitality of some formidable boarding house landlady in Morecambe, and on reflection, they deserve to suffer a bit of that. According to my chief this project was just a trial run to get foreign agents into the country to check out our coastal defence systems, military installations, airfields and so on. Customs and immigration had tightened up on the normal ports of entry and the Germans, with a bit of Irish help, were developing alternatives. It might have helped if we'd known all this earlier, of course, but it's always the same, the people in the front line are the last to know what's going in."

They'd been in the saloon bar for about ten minutes when Jack's Uncle Joss walked in. He had a smile and a word for all the regulars at the bar, and then he joined his nephew's group at their table. He insisted on buying another round of drinks.

"Thanks to all of you," he said looking round the table. "Good health, and here's a toast to you." He held up his glass, "The 'Three Men of Gragareth' ".

He laughed loudly nodding at Mike, Bob and Jack, rather pleased with his own little joke.

"Hear, hear," said Ruth enthusiastically, "to the Three Men!"

They laughed, drank and chatted with great conviviality until interrupted by the Stationmaster's appearance in the doorway.

"Miss Lancaster, a telephone call for you."

"Right, thank you Mr. Winterburn, excuse me, gentlemen."

"Grand lass, Ruth," his uncle remarked in an aside to Jack as they watched her slim figure glide out of the room.

"Aye, she is that," Jack agreed, looking closely at his uncle.

"Happen you'll get chance to see her in London, eh?" He added, ostensibly busy with the lighting of his pipe.

He's a crafty old devil, thought Jack. He laughed out loud, "It's quite possible, Uncle. We're travelling to Leeds together this afternoon and then down to London on Monday."

They chatted about the farm for a while and moved on to talk about the deteriorating political situation in Europe. Bob was adamant that there would be a war before the year was out, and the others, with the events of the last week fresh in their minds, thought he was probably right. For a man who lived in such an isolated situation his uncle was very well-informed on current affairs. It was often the case, Jack thought, there seemed to be more time to think about the things that mattered living in the country than in towns. He supposed it was all the distractions and diverse opportunities for entertainment there were in the towns. He was thinking about this when Ruth returned. Much of the anxiety had gone from her face, Jack noticed, and she seemed altogether more relaxed.

"That was another department on the phone," Ruth explained when she had sat down again. "Would you believe it? They want a full written report by Monday afternoon. You can help me with that Jack," she said smiling at him.

"It'll be a pleasure," he answered gallantly, returning her smile.

"I suppose we'd better get back to the farm, and say goodbye to Aunt Dorcas and collect our belongings." Jack said when they'd emptied their glasses. "Do you fancy walking up, Ruth?"

"Oh, I'd love to. We've got time haven't we?"

"Yes," Jack answered," a couple of hours at least before the train leaves. Will you be here, Mike, when we get back?"

"Yes, I'll see you both before you go. I'll have to make a start on some paper work."

"And I'll go and see if there's any dinner ready," Bob said as he struggled to his feet," eating one-handed takes me twice as long, you know."

Twenty Four

Langham, Yorkshire Dales, 8th July 1939

The stroll up to the farm on that sunny afternoon was one of the most blissful times Jack had ever experienced. It was the fulfilment of his dreams; they walked hand in hand up the track through the woods, paused by the lake to watch the waterfowl and, without any feeling of self-consciousness, tenderly embraced and kissed in the shade of a willow tree. Underneath this leafy umbrella the shafts of sunlight danced in Ruth's hair and with her warm body close to his own, Jack thought that this place was the nearest he would ever get to heaven, now, or in the future. They moved on reluctantly, both unwilling to leave the magic of the moment and the beauty of the place.

"What a beautiful day," Ruth murmured into Jack's neck as they strolled along the water's edge, unwilling to break, even momentarily, this all-consuming romantic attachment which united them. "Why do we suffer all the rush and bustle of London, Jack, when there are places like this in the country?"

"It's something I often think about. I've always enjoyed living up here." He thought for a moment before continuing. "It comes down to a question of priorities, I think. Getting on in the world, whatever that means... or self-fulfilment. Whether you want to live, or just exist."

That seemed to give them both a lot to think about because they were silent for a long time. Not uncomfortably silent, by any means, because their arms were still entwined, and it could be safely assumed that their thoughts also were very much attuned.

Aunt Dorcas was sorry to see them go but she cheered up considerably when Jack promised that he would spend Christmas at the farm. He shyly suggested to Ruth that she might like to come as well; and both Jack and his Aunt were overjoyed when she agreed.

At Ruth's request they returned to the village by the track which cut across the hillside. The height gave her an opportunity to look across the valley towards towards Long Lane and the limestone scars behind. In spite of her unfortunate introduction to the area she was beginning to feel a close affinity to its people and their simple lifestyle. She was astute enough, however, to realise that Jack's presence had more than a little to do with the former.

From their conversation they realised that they had many common interests, not least of which was their great love of the countryside and outdoor pastimes. Jack discovered that Ruth was quite knowledgeable about the Scottish Highlands, whereas his experience was limited to the Lake District and the Yorkshire Dales. Apparently Ruth had camped and walked extensively in Scotland; predictably her enthusiasm soon inspired Jack to suggest that it would be a good idea to explore that area together the following year. The pressure of her hand on his, and her immediate enthusiasm for the trip, elevated Jack's spirits to the stratospheric. To say he walked on air for the rest of the way hardly described his feelings at all, he wasn't aware that his feet touched anything, he seemed to float down the valley on a euphoric cloud.

Mike and Bob were waiting at the station when they arrived. They smiled a greeting but Jack could see from Mike's face that something was troubling him.

"They've found the bodies of the two soldiers who were in the GPV", he said solemnly. "They were in a ditch at the side of the road, both shot in the head. It appears that they left here and went for a drink in one of the pubs where they had the misfortune to meet up with the villains who'd held your uncle prisoner in the cave."

"They also found the body of the other soldier just off the Turbary Road when they went to pick up Lieutenant Percival," added Bob.

"So that means the army lost seven men altogether," Mike went on in a low voice. "And that Irishman, O'Brady, was largely responsible. I'm staying on here for a few more days to try and find out a bit more about him and Bergman, and where they went."

Shortly before the Leeds train arrived Jack's Uncle appeared from the Flying Dutchman with Harold Winterburn, and the whole group moved on to the platform to say goodbye to Ruth and Jack. They shook hands all round, sorry to be leaving people with whom they had shared so much in such a short time. Mike and Jack agreed to meet in London as soon as Mike had finished his enquiries up here. The danger and adversity they had shared had cemented their friendship to a degree which neither wished to lose.

Ruth and Jack settled in the first empty compartment they came to and leaned out of the window to wave to their friends as the train pulled out of the station.

They sat facing each other by the window and as the train gathered speed they looked into each other's eyes contentedly.

"You wouldn't fancy a cup of tea or coffee, would you, Ruth?" enquired Jack, a mischievous glint in his eye.

"I would not", laughed Ruth. "You just stay where you are, Jack Warrendale, you're not losing me like that again".

Epilogue

The remains of the Germans who had been killed were quietly laid to rest in the picturesque churchyard in Langham. No official mention was ever made of the event, and the story never appeared in the press. Local people had their own opinions and, as in most areas of their lives, they kept them to themselves and within the confines of the village community.

The bodies of the British soldiers were returned to their families and buried with full military honours in local cemeteries. Their next-of-kin received an official letter from the War Office informing them, with deep regret, that their loved-one had died by tragic accident whilst on special manoeuvres in the service of King and Country. The word 'special' adding an inflated distinction to their loss and was highly treasured in later years.

The ancient grey-walled church in the village of Elmet-in-Barwick, near Harrogate, was crowded for the funeral of Second Lieutenant Nigel Henry Percival, 1st Battalion, West Yorkshire Regiment. His dress sword and spurs rested together with his cap on the Union Flag draped over the coffin. The Guard of Honour, stiffly immobile, heads bowed and rifles reversed, formed the corners of a statuesque tabloid by the chancel steps. Family and friends, members of the Town Council, the village elders, the Brigadier, the Commanding Officer and fellow officers of the regiment, the High Sheriff of the County, the Chief Constable and such local dignitaries who deemed such occasions to be social necessities listened in sombre silence to the words of His Grace the Archbishop of York, a family friend,

"At the going down of the sun he passed away.

And we, in the morning will remember him. Amen."

Bunty, the adorable daughter of Lady Caroline Wentworth, her attention brought back by the congregation's response, had thought the service very moving. She eased her veil to one side and with a delicate white hand dabbed her eyes with a black lace handkerchief, once again exchanging glances with that rather dashing young cavalry officer she'd met at the Fearnley Hunt Ball at the weekend.

On the 3rd of September 1939, just six weeks after this sad occasion, Britain declared war on Germany and many thousands of people throughout the world were called upon to make a similar sacrifice. In most cases their deaths were not recognised to the same extent as that of the young subaltern who had died on the bleak slopes of Gragareth, but their sacrifice was, nonetheless, as important to each of them.

That weird vehicle, the GPV, paradoxically tested more by the enemy than by the allies on this operation, distinguished itself on the field of battle during the next five years and in most military engagements throughout the world thereafter. The word 'jeep' became a recognised part of the English language and over the next fifty years the vehicle attained legendary status and revolutionised all-terrain travel in both recreational and military circles.

On that day in early September, Jack Warrendale, clerk in the company of Thos. Beddows Ltd., Clerkenwell, had immediately decided to join up; his intention being to enlist in the army as his father had done twenty-five years earlier. Jack had arranged to see Ruth at the weekend and was waiting to discuss the matter with her before he actually signed on. However, these plans were radically altered on the Friday morning when he received an official buff-coloured envelope stamped URGENT OHMS and addressed to him personally. It was a letter from a Major Mike Bannerman, Special Operations Executive, inviting Jack to a meeting at the War Office on the following Thursday to discuss a matter of supreme national importance.

The author lives in West Yorkshire close to the Yorkshire Dales National Park and within easy reach of the Pennines. He is keen on most sports, fell walking and cycling and has a great affection for the natural world and its conservation. Classical music has always been an interest. He has travelled extensively throughout the world, mostly to remote and mountainous regions, but always enjoys coming home, meeting friends in the local and spending time with the family.

Books by the same author :

A Dales Companion & Other Stories

The Dogmatists

The Golfing Society

Further details available online at http://www.normanharrison.co.uk.